S0-CWT-514

M

Bagby, George
    I could have died

I Could Have Died

By George Bagby

I COULD HAVE DIED
GUARANTEED TO FADE
BETTER DEAD
THE TOUGH GET GOING
INNOCENT BYSTANDER
MY DEAD BODY
TWO IN THE BUSH
KILLER BOY WAS HERE
HONEST RELIABLE CORPSE
ANOTHER DAY—ANOTHER
  DEATH
CORPSE CANDLE
DIRTY POOL
MYSTERIOUSER AND
  MYSTERIOUSER
MURDER'S LITTLE HELPER
EVIL GENIUS
THE REAL GONE GOOSE
THE THREE-TIME LOSERS
DEAD WRONG
COP KILLER
DEAD STORAGE
A DIRTY WAY TO DIE
THE BODY IN THE BASKET
DEAD DRUNK

GIVE THE LITTLE CORPSE A
  GREAT BIG HAND
THE CORPSE WITH STICKY
  FINGERS
SCARED TO DEATH
DEATH AIN'T COMMERCIAL
BLOOD WILL TELL
COFFIN CORNER
DROP DEAD
IN COLD BLOOD
THE STARTING GUN
THE TWIN KILLING
THE ORIGINAL CARCASE
DEAD ON ARRIVAL
MURDER CALLING "50"
RED IS FOR KILLING
HERE COMES THE CORPSE
THE CORPSE WORE A WIG
THE CORPSE WITH THE
  PURPLE THIGHS
BIRD WALKING WEATHER
MURDER ON THE NOSE
MURDER HALF-BAKED
RING AROUND A MURDER
MURDER AT THE PIANO
BACHELORS' WIFE

I Could Have Died

GEORGE BAGBY

PUBLISHED FOR THE CRIME CLUB BY

DOUBLEDAY & COMPANY, INC.

GARDEN CITY, NEW YORK

1979

All of the characters in this book
are fictitious, and any resemblance
to actual persons, living or dead,
is purely coincidental.

Library of Congress Cataloging in Publication Data

Stein, Aaron Marc, 1906–
I could have died.

I. Title.
PZ3.S819Iad [PS3569.T34]   813'.5'2
ISBN: 0-385-14987-5
Library of Congress Catalog Card Number 78-20005

For
Billie
with love
and
in gratitude for her
patience

I Could Have Died

I

There had been no doorman, nobody out front to take Alexandra's luggage. Since this was the Sandringham, I'd assumed there would be someone. It wasn't till after I'd paid the cabbie and he'd taken off that I began to realize there was not going to be anybody. Maybe that should have alerted me. Hindsight might say that I should have been wary of picking up the bags myself and escorting Alexandra into the lobby, but it was, after all, four o'clock in the morning. Alexandra was white with exhaustion, and I was pretty well beat myself. It had been a long, tedious, uncomfortable night.

If I was thinking of anything, it was only that I wanted to get her checked in and delivered to her room as quickly as possible. It was what at that time she needed the most. For myself I was thinking that this was it, only a few minutes more and I could call it duty done and take myself to my own bed.

So far as I can remember, I'd never been inside the place before. I knew about it, of course, and its facade was familiar enough. I'd passed it countless times. That stretch of Fifth Avenue across from the park is well known even to brief-visit out-of-towners, and I'm no out-of-towner. I live in Manhattan.

As New York hotels go, the Sandringham is relatively small. It's the kind of place you don't expect to read about unless it's in the society pages. There it's likely to be characterized as "exclusive." Exclusive, in case you don't know, means you'll be excluded unless you're prepared to pay phenomenal sums for a night's lodging. At Sandringham prices you have good reason to assume that you will be supplied with every luxury and with all kinds of service.

But at four o'clock in the morning? Even in the original Sandringham across the ocean it's not impossible that by such an hour all the ladies- and gentlemen-in-waiting will have given up waiting and taken themselves to their rest. After all, we knew what it had been like out at Kennedy when Alexandra's much delayed flight had finally set down not much short of three o'clock. To describe the airport as it was at that hour would be to plagiarize Oliver Goldsmith.

Even if I'd had any forebodings, and I can't pretend that I did have, they would hardly have stopped me. It would already have been too late. Alexandra had picked up a couple of her bags and had gone on in while I'd been paying off the cabbie. There could be nothing else for it but that I pick up the rest of her luggage and follow her into the lobby.

The lobby seemed to be empty but for one clerk behind the reception desk and Alexandra at the desk.

"Mrs. Gordon," she was saying. "Mrs. Roger Gordon. I have a reservation. I know I'm very late, but that's the stupid airline and the stupid weather. Don't tell me you've given my room away. The airline people said they'd called you and let you know I was being delayed."

The clerk just stood there, slack-mouthed and pop-eyed. He wasn't speaking, and he was making no move to check her in. He could have been an idiot deaf-mute, or at least a man in the grip of some sudden seizure. With a few sour thoughts about Sandringham service, I started to step forward. I was going to have to do what I could toward spurring the man into action.

I was stopped by a voice. It came from behind me.

"This way, mister," it said, "and you, too, Mrs. Gordon. Just come along quietly and nobody gets hurt. Straight ahead and through that door to the right."

I glanced back over my shoulder. I saw the man. I saw the gun he had leveled at me. So far as I could tell from his stance and the way he held the gun, he looked capable. The sound of him, furthermore, went with the look. His speech was clear. His voice was flat, cool, and steady. He didn't sound nervous, and I was telling myself that much was good. When a man is holding a gun on you and his finger is curled around the trigger, you don't want him jumpily out of control.

I had nothing to go on but the steadiness of his hand and the tone of his voice. I couldn't see his face. My first impression was that where he should have had a head, he had, instead, an oversized parsnip with eye holes. If you're one of the lucky types who's never seen a man who is concealing his face with a nylon stocking pulled down over his head, you'll have to take my word for it. It converts a head into a vaguely shaped blob that comes to a point on top.

Turning back to Alexandra, I now saw a second parsnip head. This one had joined the clerk behind the desk.

"You heard the man, Mrs. Gordon," he said. His voice

was a soft purr. "You just go on into the bar. You'll check in later. I'm sorry there's no bar service this time of night, but you can be comfortable in there."

Meanwhile my man was talking to me.

"Into the bar," he said. "Nice and quiet and peaceful. When we get in there, you'll lie down on the floor and take your pants off."

I loved Alexandra dearly, but never for her mind. In fairness to her I suppose I should say that from where she stood she couldn't see the gun trained on my spine. The parsnip who'd materialized behind the counter hadn't pulled a gun on her, but it probably would have made no difference even if she'd have known the threat was there. That was Alexandra. She had to speak up.

"This," she said, "is no time to play stupid games. We've had a hideous night. Mr. Bagby's been out at the airport hours and hours waiting for my stupid plane to come in, and I've been stuck at O'Hare for hours and hours and hours waiting for my stupid plane to take off, and we're neither of us in the mood for stupid jokes."

"This is no joke, Mrs. Gordon," her parsnip said.

"Then it's robbery," Alexandra said, and that was quick of her. "Let me tell you then. You're making a mistake. You're making the mistake of your lives. Maybe you don't know who Mr. Bagby is, but you can take my word for it. He isn't just anybody. His best friend is Inspector Schmidt and everybody knows who Inspector Schmidt is. Mr. Bagby and the Police Department, they're that close. You can't be so stupid that you want the inspector after you. You mess with the inspector's friend, and you're in trouble. Inspector Schmidt is Chief of Homicide."

"No homicide, Mrs. Gordon," the parsnip said. "But thanks for telling me." He called across to my parsnip.

"Take them inside," he ordered, "but let this one keep his pants on."

"But . . ."

The man behind the desk was not stopping for argument.

"He's Mr. Bagby," he said. "For Mr. Bagby I have plans. I want him with his pants on."

We were herded into the bar. We had company in there. There was, of course, a third parsnip head standing guard with a gun. We were turned over to him and the word was passed that I was to keep my pants on. Except for Alexandra there was no woman in there, just four men under the gun. They were all without pants, but from the rest of their uniforms I knew them. The big guy in the jacket with the tasseled epaulets would have to be the doorman. The two with the brass buttons and the pillbox hats were, obviously, bellboys. The starched white shirt, black tie, and dinner jacket would be another desk clerk. At sight of Alexandra they all took to tugging at shirts and the bottoms of jackets and tunics, trying for the maximum possible concealment. The doorman and the clerk weren't bad off. They had shirt tails and reasonably long jackets. The bellboys had nothing below the waist. At sight of Alexandra they wailed.

She yawned elaborately.

"Not to worry," she said. "I've been traveling all night. I'm dead for sleep. I can't possibly keep my eyes open."

She turned her back on the squirming bellboys and gave all her attention to me.

"Poor George," she said. "After you've been so sweet and waited all that time to meet me, now this. You shouldn't have waited, you know. It was much beyond the call of duty. I expect you'll never do that again, though I must say I can't be sorry you're here. This would be horrid if I were alone."

I had no idea of what she might say next. I scowled at her in the hope she would get the message and shut up. She got the message, but I should have known. It didn't shut her up.

"There's no reason why we shouldn't talk," she said. "It doesn't matter if they do hear us. After all, aren't you glad I spoke up and told them who you were. If I hadn't, you'd be down there on the floor with those poor men. It's only because of me that they are letting you keep your pants on."

It was no good reminding her that the man had said he had plans for me. I'd been trying to tell myself that plans for me with my pants on were likely to be preferable to plans for me with my pants off, but I couldn't work up any noticeable preference for any sort of plans the man might be making for me. It was more than possible that, short of gagging her, she would go on talking no matter what I did; but it was a certainty that anything I might say would only serve to keep her going. If forced to it, Alexandra could do a monologue. Her preference, however, was for conversational give and take.

What she had said, furthermore, was enough. The parsnip head riding herd on us had been told that I was to keep my pants on and nothing more than that. Alexandra's saying that I might have been down on the floor with the others woke him up. He hadn't been told that I was to be allowed to sit on a bar stool. He was quick to set things right.

"Get down there," he ordered. "Get down there with the rest of them guys."

I was working hard at registering on everything I could

observe and on ticketing it away in my memory. As I got off the bar stool and lay down on the floor, I was thinking that here I had a little something. The two outside had both been well spoken. This one was ungrammatical. Although his was street speech, however, it was not New York street speech. It had been "them guys" and not "dem guys."

Of course Alexandra went to bat for me. She was never one to let a friend down. She was never one to keep her mouth shut. Since this parsnip head had not been out in the lobby when she had warned the other pair of my eminence, she now seemed to think it was no more than fair that she should warn this one as well. So she did it all over again for him. This time it got her nothing but a laugh.

"You're scaring me to death, lady," the lug said.

"My good man," Alexandra began. She broke off to drop in an aside. "I don't know why I call him that," she said, "since it's obvious that nothing could be farther from the truth, but then what else is there to call him?" Resuming her argument, she made a fresh start. "My good man," she said, "your associates outside showed better sense. They got the message. The man outside said it plainly. Mr. Bagby is to have special treatment. You will do well to face facts. This childish bravado can do you no good."

She would have gone on with it and, I believe, much in the same vein, but at that point whatever she might have been saying was drowned out. The parsnip who had escorted Alexandra and me into the bar had now returned, and he was chivvying another captive ahead of him. This one was saying nothing, but at sight of her the bellhops broke out in noisy wails of protest. If being in Alexandra's presence had upset them, the arrival now of another woman had them in a frenzy.

You must understand about Alexandra. I might say that she had come to me by inheritance. She had been my mother's best friend. Among my earliest memories were those occasions when she had perched me on her knee and, engulfing me in her perfume, she would feed me those spectacular things otherwise unknown to the diet of my preschool years—*marrons glacés*, sugared violets, *madeleines, bouchée de Noël.*

By that night when I'd met her much-delayed plane, my mother had many years before come to the end of a long life. Alexandra, however, although her contemporary, had survived. She was seemingly indestructible. Since for as long as I could remember her age had been always "over twenty-one"—or had been until the voting age had been reduced and Alexandra, as was her wont, had changed with the times and that night was "over eighteen"—and one could make one's own guess at which side of ninety that "over eighteen" might fall.

Though hotel bellboys are boys in name only, the unhappy pair beside me on the floor were young enough, certainly not yet out of their twenties and therefore of an age that would have made them the contemporaries of Alexandra's great-great-grandsons if she'd had any such.

Now, however, there was this newcomer being forced into our company. The newcomer was female. She was beautiful. She was also young, hardly as young as those debagged bellhops but certainly no more than ten years their senior, if as much as that. She had a pale cashmere topcoat slung across her shoulders, and she was wearing it as though it were a cape. It took her no more than the quickest glance to come to terms with the situation and no more than a moment to act on it. Even as she was crossing to the bar, she pulled the coat from her shoulders and, in passing, she dropped it over the two bellhops, providing them with cover.

"Good morning," she said, mounting a bar stool alongside Alexandra.

Alexandra beamed at her.

"Good morning, my dear," she said. "May I say that just in a single moment you have changed all my preconceptions about your generation?"

"For the better I hope."

"That was a kind and thoughtful act. At the risk of sounding old-fashioned—a risk which at my age I should be most careful not to take—it was the act of a lady."

"I'm warm enough without it. They need it more than I do."

"Nevertheless," Alexandra persisted, "a unisex Sir Walter Raleigh."

If from that you're shaping up a picture of anything even fractionally masculine, forget it. Good as the newcomer had been with the coat draped around her, she was even better without it. She was wearing black slacks and a black silk shirt, essentially mannish garments, but what she did for them was far beyond the compass of any man.

She offered Alexandra her hand.

"Jane Harcourt," she said.

Alexandra took the proferred hand.

"Alexandra Gordon," she said, "and that's George Bagby at your feet. He's the one in mufti and in pants. Of course, he was forced down there by that faceless imbecile with the gun; but faceless imbecile or no, I can promise you he would have been at your feet in any case. I suppose you know that you're extraordinarily beautiful, my dear."

"I know that I'm extraordinarily inconvenienced. All of us are. This is wearing; but what's worse, it's so ugly. They look horrible with those stockings over their heads. It could just as easily have been amusing masks."

Alexandra shrugged.

"It speaks to what they are," she said, "to their sense of values. Evidently it's a robbery, and they are devoid of even rudimentary taste. Just for mere money they convert themselves into these amorphous blobs."

I very much doubted that our guard would have any understanding of "amorphous," but it was quite possible that "blob" would not be beyond him. It worried me, but there wasn't much I could do about it. I could only lie there at the feet of the two proud beauties and fret. He did take umbrage.

"You dames talk too much," he said. "Button your lip."

"Oh, come, my good man," Alexandra began. She broke off to explain to her new friend. "I keep calling him that," she said. "Silly, isn't it? But it's just force of habit."

"Try 'my good blob,'" Jane suggested.

Alexandra returned to the parsnip head.

"As I was about to say, you cannot expect that we will just sit here and be bored. After all, you might take into consideration that we are behaving very well. It's a dreadful hour, and we are being kept from our rest. We're not weeping or whimpering, we're not being disagreeable, we're making no fuss. This is the way civilized people behave. Certainly, in consideration of what we are putting up with and, if I may say so, with good grace, it is not too much to ask that you put up with us."

"Yeah, missus, I'm not asking nothing. I'm holding the gun and I'm telling."

Alexandra sighed.

"Perhaps it would be best," she said, "if you put all your faculties into holding the gun and didn't try to say anything. You are clearly not up to doing both."

. Jane giggled.

"I thought this was going to be a bore," she said. "But if it weren't for the blobs, we would never have met, and you're marvelous. I wouldn't have missed you for anything."

"It would have been just as well if you had missed this," Alexandra said.

"No," Jane replied. "This is fun, and I would have missed it, if it hadn't been for my insomnia. I woke at two and just couldn't get back to sleep, and there I was without even something to read. I just had to get up and dress and get out of that damn room upstairs. I had the silly idea I'd go to an all-night movie."

Alexandra was fascinated.

"One of those Forty-second Street places where all the films are called *Babes in Bondage* or *Teen-age Trollops?* Did you go? Tell me. What was it like?"

"I went and it was dreadful. It was smelly and crawly. If I didn't pick up fleas, it will be a miracle. Then a man moved to the seat beside me and he started pressing my knee, and that wasn't the least bit amusing. He was bald and he had a nauseating case of bad breath. I pulled away and came back here."

"Just in time," Alexandra said.

"Yes. If I'd been able to sleep, I'd have been upstairs and missed the whole thing. Or if that movie house hadn't been so disgusting, I would have stayed on through the picture, and again I'd have missed all this. It's the most exciting thing that's ever happened to me."

They went on and on, tossing the conversational ball back and forth. They might have been two Alexandras, both of them so above it all that they had me almost feeling sorry for our fuming guard. At least I was assuming that he was fuming. I could well imagine that he was going red in the face and from red to purple as his blood pressure took the high road to apoplexy. It was all a guess, of course, because with the stocking over his head there was no knowing. His color didn't show through the nylon. He gave up on them and just let them go on with their chatter, and go on with it they did. With each successive exchange they rose to new heights of outrageousness.

They tried to draw me into their conversational give and take, but I was having none of that. I have no special talent for improvising drawing-room comedy, and in the face of a revolver I had no wish to.

It didn't matter. The ladies did well enough without me. They got on to hairdressers and health farms, fashions and fads. They came around to husbands. Alexandra had had four. Jane was still to have her first.

"You must know what you want and go after it," I remember hearing Alexandra advise. "Go after it. Grab it, and no regrets—never any regrets. My four, they were darlings all of them. I could have gone through my whole life with any one of them and happily, but by the very nature of things, it was not to be. They were lovely men, but they never had any permanence in them."

"Inconstant? I can't believe that. No man would ever leave you. For what, Alexandra, for whom?"

"Oh, never unfaithful, my dear child. They were exciting men, reckless men. They lived dangerously and one after the other, they died of it."

She ran through the history of her marriages, or more exactly the story of how each of the unions came to an end.

"I go back so far," she said, "that my first husband had to find a way to kill himself without the aid of an internal-combustion engine. It was a horse. Jasper was thrown and died instantly of a broken neck. For Stephen it was the first war. He couldn't wait for this country to get into it. He was off to the Lafayette Escadrille. He was shot down in flames. Wilbur was really too old for the second war, but that was something he just couldn't accept. He wangled his way into the army and then wangled his way into combat. They told me that his bravery was an inspiration to the younger officers. I've wondered how many of them he inspired to do as he did, get themselves killed." She sighed, but if there was a moment of sadness, she threw it off. "That leaves Roger," she said. "He always drove too fast and too brilliantly. It was inevitable that one day he would meet someone on the road who drove just as fast but less brilliantly. The inevitable is like that. It cannot fail to happen."

"And a steady, cautious type who might have lasted all your life wouldn't have been as much fun."

"A steady, cautious type would never have suited me at all. I had fireworks, mad music, excitement, and with it all, inevitable heartbreak. The heart, my dear, mends and will be whole again, but stifle it with boredom and it may never recover. So it's the choice one makes. If the steady and even course should be for you, then lucky you. But if it's the ups and downs, the highs and the lows, the ecstasy and the loss, then even luckier you."

Jane laughed.

"That's for me," she said, "but no luck. I never meet any exciting men. Could it be that there are no more? Maybe you had them all, Alexandra."

Alexandra laughed with her.

"You make me sound greedy," she said.

"Not at all," Jane said. "Just bring an exciting one my way. I'll grab and no regrets."

There was a lot more of it. They never even for a moment ran down. I drifted from only half listening to blotting out their chatter completely. On the sounds coming through from the lobby I had a good enough idea of what was happening out there. The parsnip heads were working on the hotel safe and the safe-deposit boxes. Similar capers had been pulled off in other hotels of the Sandringham class. In each case the haul had been impressive. On almost any night the cash and the jewels left in hotel safekeeping by patrons of such top-bracket hostelries are likely to run into millions. Make it the night of one of the big society balls when Texans and other such, in town for the event, return from the festivities and deposit the emeralds and diamonds and rubies in the safe for overnight security, then the millions multiply. I was trying to think whether this had been such a night, but I had to give up on that. I was telling myself that it might well have been. The parsnip heads obviously would be more studious readers of the society pages than I could ever be.

I couldn't believe that they were going to settle for nothing more than just robbing the safe. It seemed far more likely that, once they were at it, they would be doing the total job, and that would mean hitting Alexandra and Jane and me for anything we might have on us.

I wasn't going to be good for much: only my watch, cuff links, and the small amount of cash I had left on me after I'd paid off the airport cab. We live in a credit-card world where it is considered the better part of wisdom to keep on one's person a reasonable quantity of unnecessary cash just to keep a possible mugger from being violently unhappy. Many's the victim who has suffered serious injury at the hands of a savage and disappointed mugger. No few have even come to death at such hands.

I was trying to calculate how much cash I still had on me after paying off the cabbie. It would have been quite enough for tipping the boys who might have handled Alexandra's luggage and for getting myself the short distance to my own place. I was very much afraid that for keeping a mugger happy and nonviolent, it would be grossly insufficient.

Alexandra, I was certain, they would find not much less unsatisfactory. In her life there had always been one man or another to pick up the tab. It was an easy guess that there would be nothing in her purse that wasn't a great deal less than the cost of the purse itself. There would be her check book and her credit cards, but in the negotiable no more than some paltry few dollars. There were, of course, her rings. The wedding band and the diamond on the third finger of her left hand were in plain view.

In her luggage there would be three more wedding bands and three more diamond rings. Several years earlier she had revolted against the burden and the worry of owning costly jewelry. I had a clear memory of her telling me of her decision.

"It's always seemed the height of folly," she said. "But when you have a husband you adore and he gives you these things, you can't hurt his feelings by being sensible about them. After Jasper's death I sold everything—not, of course, my wedding band or engagement ring. They were different, and even when I'd married Stephen and I was wearing his, I still kept Jasper's."

And that had been the pattern. Now with Roger gone and no successor, the wedding band and the diamond she was wearing were still his; but, as she'd done three times before, she had sold all other jewelry Roger had given her.

Apart from the gold band and the one diamond she had on her and the three similar pairs of keepsakes from her earlier marriages that would be in her luggage, there would be nothing on her person or in her suitcases but costume jewelry. Since all four of the diamonds were sizable stones of good quality, I was thinking that the parsnips wouldn't disdain them.

I was also thinking, however, that it was going to be most painful for Alexandra if she was to be forced to part with them. What Jane's situation might be, I couldn't even guess. She was wearing no jewelry, not even any costume stuff, and she wasn't carrying a handbag. It was possible, of course, that she had been stripped of anything she had on her before they'd brought her into the bar; but, since neither Alexandra nor I had been handled in that fashion, it seemed unlikely.

The two men outside in the lobby had been firm but not violent. The one standing guard over us in the bar was an ugly type, and I didn't know how many more there might be or what they might be like. I was still trying to add up the possibilities when two of them came into the bar, herding before them the clerk who had been behind the desk. Their entrance brought my count of parsnip heads up to four. One of them we had encoun-

tered earlier. He appeared to be the head parsnip. He was
the one who'd said he had plans for me. The other, however, was not the man who had come up behind me with
the gun. This bucko was bigger and huskier. I'm not
suggesting that any of them looked to be weaklings, but
this one was conspicuously taller, heavier, and burlier
than the others.

At sight of me, head turnip was apologetic.

"Mr. Bagby," he said. "Please get up. No need for you
to be down there on the floor. I thought I'd made that
clear, but I suppose I wasn't explicit enough. Please get
up and just wait with the ladies. We'll not be long now."

I got to my feet and perched on a bar stool. There was
nothing else for it. We'd been under the gun all along, but
now there were two revolvers trained on us. The big muscle man had a third one, but he had his tucked into his
belt. He was keeping both of his formidable paws free.
From his left he had several leather straps dangling.

The four hotel employees lying on the floor eyed the
straps and moaned in unison. The head parsnip turned to
the clerk he'd just brought in.

"You'll oblige me by taking your pants off and joining
the others on the floor," he said. "You can take the place
Mr. Bagby just left."

The clerk started to protest. Head parsnip cut him off.

"You have been sensible and co-operative so far," he
said. "Now, when we are almost finished here, is no time
to begin being difficult. You've had no choice and you've
understood that. You still have no choice. If you won't
take them off, my friend here will take them off you. I'd
like him to be gentle, but I don't deceive myself about
him. You'll be wise to do as I do—don't deceive yourself
about him."

He indicated with the inclination of his parsnip head his friend, the muscles with the handful of straps.

The unhappy clerk skinned out of his pants and started lowering himself to the floor. He was stopped.

"Like the others. You're no exception. Shorts off as well."

Up to that point the man had been white in the face. Now he flushed crimson. Holding his shirt tails down with one hand, he pulled off his shorts with the other. Then it was a laborious process getting down to the floor. Hanging on to everything in an effort to keep himself covered, he went down by stages, first falling to his knees and then going the rest of the way. The ladies all the while couldn't have been more ladylike. They averted their heads and shut their eyes.

"Good," head parsnip said. He turned to the big hulk with the straps. "They're yours," he told the man. "You know what to do."

The moans swelled into wails of protest. The big guy ignored them and went to work. Taking the men one after the other, he worked quickly and efficiently. It was two straps to a man. One went around the ankles and one trussed the arms tight to the man's sides. He began with the doorman, perhaps because he was physically the most prepossessing of the lot. The man made one small move toward resistance, but that was quickly knocked off by a savage lash of the strap across the man's bared calves.

That was all it took. The rest was easy. The doorman held still and the others, eyeing the angry welt that had come up on the doorman's legs, offered themselves almost eagerly for the trussing up. Each of them in addition was secured to the anchored support of a bar stool. They were carefully spaced so that none was in touching reach of another. While the straps were being secured, parsnip-in-charge talked to them.

"Someone may come along quickly and turn you loose," he said. "It is also possible that there will be no one until daylight. Whenever it is, you will, of course, lose no time in calling the police. We can't expect anything else. When you do call the police, it is imperative that you tell them that, when we left here, we took Mrs. Gordon, Miss Harcourt, and Mr. Bagby with us. We shall be holding them as hostages as long as we consider it necessary. The police, of course, will be hearing from them as soon as we have released them. Until such time, the police must realize that any unwise police action will threaten the lives of these three most attractive people. It may be of interest to the police to know that Mr. Bagby is Mr. George Bagby who, I am told, has friends on the force, his special friend being Inspector Schmidt, Chief of Homicide." He turned to Alexandra. "I do have that right, Mrs. Gordon, don't I?"

Alexandra glared at him.

"You're disappointing me," she said. "You have so much style. I expected better of you. You couldn't have chosen a more stupid course."

"Allow me to know better than you, Mrs. Gordon," he said. "I'd never presume to call myself your superior in anything else, but here, in this, I am your superior in experience."

"Experience, nonsense," Alexandra said. "Anyone knows the penalty for kidnapping is much heavier than for robbery."

"Anyone knows that," the man conceded, "but experience tells us something else. Penalties are exacted for only one thing and for nothing else, and that one thing is get-

ting caught. We are not going to get caught. I am arranging for that."

"Could you be persuaded to take just me and let the ladies go?" I asked.

I had little expectation that he would go for it, but I
had to make the try. Before he could answer Alexandra
was in there protesting. Obviously, it had come through
to her that her babbling about Inspector Schmidt may
have put ideas into the parsnip head. So now she was
feeling responsible for me. That Jane was protesting as
well was something I could not as readily explain. It
seemed almost as though she might be afraid she was
going to miss the fun.

The head parsnip took over, and the women fell silent.

"No, Mr. Bagby," he said, "the police might just possibly be so unfeeling as to think you expendable. I can't
imagine anyone, even a policeman, considering either
Miss Harcourt or Mrs. Gordon expendable."

In the trussing up of the two bellboys Jane's coat had
been in the way. The big guy had flung it impatiently
aside, much to the evident discomfiture of the two unhappy victims. Since in their misery they were burying
their faces in the carpeting on the bar floor, they couldn't
see the Victorian modesty with which Alexandra and,
perhaps more incongruously, Jane were averting their
eyes.

Parsnip-in-charge picked the coat up off the floor, in-
spected it for dust, and flicked a few specks off it. Crossing to Jane, he put it over her shoulders. He fussed at it,
arranging it just so, and in the process giving her a tenta-
tive little squeeze. She gave no indication that she was
aware of it. He stayed there at her side until he had seen

the last of the hotel people secured. Then, offering Alexandra his hand, he helped her down from her bar stool.

"I'm sure Mr. Bagby will give you his arm, Mrs. Gordon," he said.

It was too much. He might have been asking me to take
her into dinner. It was farcical, but I certainly couldn't
object to it. It was so civilized. I didn't see that I could do
any better than play along in the hope that I might help
with keeping it civilized. There were the other two—the
one who had been standing guard over us in the bar and
the big lug. Their presence was a potent reminder that at
any moment this thing could turn savage. There was also
the other man, the one who had first held the gun on me.
I remembered that he had been well spoken, but otherwise I could recall little about him that I was prepared to
call civilized.

I gave Alexandra my arm. Parsnip-in-command gave
me a small nod. Even though I couldn't read his face, I
could assume that it tokened approval. He turned to Jane
Harcourt. She was still on her bar stool. For her he had a
playful little smack on the neat curve of her bottom.

"Move it, beautiful," he said. "Time to go."

Her lips twitched. She was working at suppressing a
smile. I detected a slight look of smugness she couldn't
suppress. She moved. He took her arm. Suddenly everything went up tempo. We were hurried out to the lobby
and through the lobby doors to the street. The fourth
man, the one who had remained out in the lobby, fell in
behind us.

Each one of them seemed to know his position and precisely what he was to do. Two cars stood parked at the
curb. There was a man behind the wheel of each and
both cars had their motors running. The drivers had their

hats tilted forward over their eyes and their coat collars turned up. They weren't parsnip heads, but their faces were quite as much out of sight.

The head man and the lug who'd been guarding us in the bar rushed us across the sidewalk and into the first car. It was obvious that they wanted to keep as brief as possible these moments during which with their parsnip heads they would be exposed out on the street. I didn't know whether I should have been hoping that someone would be happening along at that unlikely time of night to see us and sound an alarm, but it didn't matter. There was no one.

They piled into the first car with us. The other pair dove into the second car and, even as the car doors were slamming shut, both cars shot away from the curb. We took the first turning and headed east. The other car didn't come after us. I took that to be the mark of professionalism, but I did have the thought that it was also the mark of trust. It hardly seemed likely that they had already made a division of the loot.

It was close in the car. Alexandra and Jane and I were in the back seat. Our two captors were on the jump seats, facing us and holding their guns on us. I concentrated on watching the streets we were taking. In almost every kidnapping I'd ever known anything about there had been every effort made to keep the victims from knowing where they were taken or from being able to locate for the police where they had been held. This one was different. They didn't seem to care.

We had swung east off Fifth Avenue and had gone all the way across to the Franklin D. Roosevelt Drive. Now we were on the Drive, headed downtown. Suddenly the head man was in trouble. He began sneezing and gasping

and strangling. We were tearing south in the left lane of
the Drive. Although he was sitting in the right-hand jump
seat, he leaned across the other man and started rolling
down the window on the left side. His own gun he'd
dropped to the floor and now, leaning across, he had himself jammed up against the other man's gun. I was never
going to have a better chance to jump them and the
chance was not going to last for more than a moment.

I was in perfect position for it at the left side of the seat
with the two men in the tangle directly in front of me.
Lunging forward, I could dump my full weight on top of
them and keep them tied up long enough for Jane to grab
up the gun from where it had dropped at her feet. I
couldn't kid myself that I could hold them for long. Everything was going to hang on whether Jane would be
quick enough to get the message. She was going to have
to have control of that loose gun before they could shove
my weight off them.

Alexandra was on the seat between us and there was no
time for getting the message across to Jane. She needed to
come to it on her own, moving along with me. It was
going to be two-minds-with-but-a-single-thought stuff. It
would be that or nothing. I started my lunge, but it got
nowhere.

In the first place it took off to a slower start than the
situation demanded. I had moved soon enough, but so
had Alexandra. She had grabbed at my arm. It was no
problem breaking away from her grasp; but, in the process, I lost that one tick. I came in on them just too late to
put my weight into holding them piled up one on the
other. In that split second the guy in the jump seat facing
me had started the powerful shove that pushed the other
guy off him. I lunged straight into his newly freed re-

volver. With the muzzle of it drilled into my belly, he drove me back hard. The other gun was still where it had fallen. As far as I could see, Jane hadn't so much as reached for it.

On the other hand its owner wasn't reaching for it either. He seemed to be strangling. Convulsed with his coughing and sneezing and sputtering and wheezing, he reached up with both his hands and tore off his nylon stocking. Flinging it away from him, he rolled down the window at his side of the car and, sticking his head out, he took great, gasping gulps of air.

I sat there tensed, waiting for him to bring his head back in. I couldn't believe that we were going to have more than a moment for seeing his face. I was determined that in such a moment I would see it and record it so solidly in my memory that forever afterward I would know it anywhere. I'd had the most fleeting glimpse of it while he had been ripping the stocking off and diving for the window, but what I'd seen then was a face so distorted in its effort to breathe that I doubted I could ever recognize it if I should see it in repose.

The other guy reached with his foot and kicked the loose gun across the car floor to where it was within his easy reach. He darted his free hand down and grabbed it up. Ramming it into his belt, he prodded my gut with the other one, the one he had been holding on me. The opportunity had been missed, and I couldn't hope for another like it. I tried to put it from my mind and to concentrate on understanding what was happening. Keeping my eyes fixed on the man where he was leaning out of the window, set on catching that moment when he would bring his head back in and I would get to see his face, I found myself coming to some sort of an understanding of what was going on.

The man was struggling under an allergic attack. It sounded and it looked like hay fever and asthma, the works. An attack of that sort can be bad enough under any circumstances. In the confinement of that nylon stocking it would obviously have been unendurable. Even in his desperate reach for air, however, the man had still remembered that sticking his masked head out of the window on his side of the car would be dangerous. At any moment a passing car might be riding alongside and the nylon stocking mask would be seen.

Since he'd been concerned about that possibility even in his agony, he'd lunged across to the window on the left-hand side of the car. We were riding in the left lane of the Drive, and we were headed downtown. That meant there was nothing on that side of the car but the barricade and beyond it the river. There could be nobody there who might possibly spot his parsnip head. Rammed back to his own side of the car, he had evidently given up on it. I was guessing that he'd realized that he'd put himself between me and his partner's gun, and he couldn't do that again. He had done the only thing that remained to him, ripped the nylon off and put his head out of the window on the side of the car where it might be seen. I could further guess that he was in such bad shape that he was past any worry about exposing his face.

After a few minutes he brought his head back in. The gasping and the wheezing had stopped, but his eyes and his nose were running water in steady streams. Even with the most frantic mopping with his soaked handkerchief he couldn't keep ahead of the flow.

"Allergy," he panted. "Perfume allergy."

"Oh, dear," Alexandra said, all sympathy. "Mine, I'm afraid."

The man nodded.

"I am sorry," Alexandra said. "I didn't know."

"Of course, you didn't."

The other man stepped into it.

"They're seeing your face," he said. "They're getting a good look at you."

"It can't be helped. I'd have drowned if I kept the damn nylon on."

"Yeah? So now what are you going to do about them?"

"Shut up."

"It's your ass, but you can't . . ."

"I told you to shut up."

He reached over and pulled his gun out of the other man's belt. The man subsided to an inarticulate mumble.

That bare face left hanging out was hardly at its best. The eyes were beyond belief bloodshot and the nose was red and puffy. The man's hair stood up in disordered spikes all over his head. It had been pulled every which way by the nylon and then blown about by the wind. His neatly trimmed mustache and his neat beard were soaked and matted with those nonstop discharges he had pouring out of his eyes and nose.

Past all that, however, I had the impression of an uncommonly handsome face. Rugged bone structure and firmness of the flesh saved it from being pretty. If you put any faith into reading character from features and expression, it struck me as a kind face and one that was humorous.

If I had the thought that actors with faces like his had

always been sought for such roles as Robin Hood or Jimmy Valentine, I need hardly explain how it came about that I should have been thinking of him in such connection.

II

Despite the problem with his allergy he was back in command. He turned around, leaving it to his partner to keep me and the ladies covered. Leaning forward, he spoke to the driver. During this bout of respiratory difficulty his speech at best wasn't too clear. Since he was speaking into the driver's ear and holding his voice low, I couldn't catch anything of what he was saying. Whatever it was, the driver didn't like it.

"You're crazy," the driver said.

Then there was something more I couldn't catch. From the driver's response to it, however, it was easy to guess what it had been.

"You're goddamn right it's your ass," he said.

Our man turned back to us. More precisely he turned to Alexandra.

"Mrs. Gordon," he said, "I'm sorry to have to do this to you." I braced myself. It seemed as though I was going to have to do something, however desperate and however hopeless. "I'd like to drop you some place where you could pick up a cab immediately. Believe me, I wish I could do that, but I hope you understand my situation. Too many people about, too little lead time between our

dropping you and your giving the alarm—I cannot take
the risk. Even if I were ready to hazard it for myself, I
have no right to take the chance for these men. You must
understand that."

I couldn't wait him out. He was driving me crazy with
all this explanation and apology.

"What are you going to do?"

"We're going to drop Mrs. Gordon off. Unhappily it
must be on a deserted street where she will have a walk
of several blocks before she can reach a telephone or find
a cab. It can't be a residential street where, even at this
hour, she could ring a bell and wake someone who will
take her in and let her use the phone. I'm planning on a
street in the wholesale furniture district. It's in the Thirties down here by the river. This time of night everything
along there is shut up tight. She won't see a soul for
blocks and blocks."

"And you're setting her up for a mugger," Jane argued.

I was saying nothing. I was hoping it was to be just as
he was describing it. It was all too possible that this was
just some soothing syrup to keep us placid until he would
be ready to act.

"I've been thinking about that," he said. "It worries
me, but it can't be helped. I'm comforting myself with the
law of averages. After all, Mrs. Gordon has already had
one encounter with nasty men tonight. Another in the one
same night is most unlikely. The law of averages is
against it."

"I always knew you was a nut," his partner said. "But
tonight you've really flipped. You can't . . ."

"I know what you're thinking. I don't want to hear it."

"You've got to hear it. You've got to make sense."

"No."

"Then I'm taking over."

I'd missed that one chance, and I'd despaired of ever having another, but now it came. The goon who was still a parsnip head swung his gun off me and rammed it into the belly of his partner. With his free hand he grabbed for the other man's gun and was wrenching it out of the man's hand. I knew what he had in mind and I knew that he had the driver with him—by the act of unmasking himself, the head man had condemned the three of us to death. Nobody was going to be turned loose to make an identification.

I had no guarantee that I could do us any good, but I had to make the try. The guy who was still masked, after all, had made the mistake of offering me the back of his neck. I accepted the target and chopped him hard. He crumpled. Our unmasked kidnapper, coming up with both the guns, waved me back into my seat. His eyes and his nose were still streaming, but he managed a smile.

"Thank you," he said. "That was nicely done. Now you can sit back and relax."

We left the river drive and turned west, back into the city, but only for a couple of blocks in the lower Thirties. That area was the warehouse and wholesale furniture district he'd specified. Even there he was choosing just the right spot. He picked a place midway between street lights, the darkest spot he could find. There he ordered the driver to pull up. Getting Alexandra out of the car was no simple matter.

For one thing, she was entering a protest. She didn't want to go without me, and just as I thought she was about to go into that old gag line, "I leave with the guy what brung me," she expanded it to include her friend, Jane, as well. The three of us were in this thing together and we were going to stay together, come what may.

"There's nothing I'd like better, Mrs. Gordon," our man told her, "but it can't be. Neither you nor I can help it, but it is your perfume. Just a little more, and it'll be the death of me."

With that he addressed himself to the physical problem of moving her out of the car without in the process losing control. She was at the center of the back seat between Jane and me. Both jump seats were occupied. He was in one of them and his now unconscious cohort was slumped in the other. Alexandra was anchored, completely hedged around with bodies.

Without even a moment's hesitation, he took the matter in hand. He ordered the driver to get out and open the door on my side of the car.

"I'll keep Mr. Bagby covered while you're hauling stupid out. Just pull him out and lay him on the sidewalk. He'll be all right."

The driver put in a protest.

"You can't leave him like that."

"We're not leaving him. It's just for a minute to get him out of the way."

Grumbling, the driver did as he was told. As the weight came off the jump seat, it flipped up out of the way.

"Now, Mrs. Gordon, please," the man said.

Alexandra wasn't moving.

"Darling," Jane said, "do go. We'll be all right. I know we'll be all right."

"It seems wrong," Alexandra said. "It was only because of me that George got into this."

Meanwhile the driver had come up with another gun. He had it trained on me. Nobody could fault their teamwork. There was going to be that little time when Alexandra would start out of the car. For a few moments then she would be between me and the other man's gun. For those few moments the driver was going to have me covered.

"My friend will come in after you, Mrs. Gordon, if he must," the man said.

So Alexandra surrendered, but not without first going through some characteristic motions. I've never known whether she was stalling in the hope that even along that dark and deserted street a police car might come prowling by, or if it was just that nothing could make her swerve from the pursuit of her inflexible code. She took the time for saying affectionate *adieux* to Jane and me, stopping to kiss first her and then me on both our cheeks.

"Start walking west," the man told her.

Since we were pulled up on a westbound street, we could see Alexandra as she walked away from us. After she had gone five or six paces, she turned to wave at us, but something strange happened to that wave. It had no more than gotten started when it hesitated and fluttered away into no gesture at all. Her shoulders slumped. As she walked on, she was the very picture of defeat.

The driver meanwhile was picking up the goon I'd knocked out. He moved to stuff the still unconscious man back into the car with us. Our man wouldn't have it.

"Take him up front with you," he said. "I'm sick of him." He turned to me. "Please shut the door, Mr. Bagby."

Having done as he was told, the driver took his place behind the wheel. Before he could start away from the curb, there was another order.

"Back out of the street and around the corner."

"What's that for?"

"Mrs. Gordon. She looked back to read the license number, but there's no plate in front. We don't| want to drive past her and give her a look at the back, do we now?"

The driver mumbled something, but he backed to the end of the street and around the corner. Alexandra's aborted wave was now explained. Poor Alexandra! She'd had a good idea, but the man had been ahead of her.

Within moments we were back on the Franklin D. Roosevelt Drive and again headed downtown. With Alexandra out of the car and the window open to the river breeze, even the lingering vestiges of her perfume were blown away. The effect was miraculous. The streaming of the man's eyes and nose just stopped. He stowed away his soaked handkerchief and became chatty.

"I have to think of everything," he said, "because they think of nothing. It's a nuisance, but it's just as well that it should be that way. When they try to think, the results are disastrous. They just can't ever think anything but muscle and lead—no subtlety, no finesse. It's the one drawback of a life of crime. It puts a man into bad company. You can never know how boring they are."

"A man like you," Jane said, "I'd think you could do better than this."

He laughed.

"Better?" he said. "This few hours' work tonight will be good for a healthy part of a million for each of us in the six-way split. That's nice money, my dear, and it's tax-free income. It even beats municipal bonds."

We came off the highway and turned west as far as Lafayette Street, but there we turned to head downtown again. I tried to figure what lay in that direction. There

would be the financial district and Little Italy and China-
town, but I could make no sense of any of those. I
thought of the Holland Tunnel and of the Jersey possibilities that lay beyond it. I also thought of the bridges
and of the broad reaches of Brooklyn. All those possibilities seemed much too far off. It could be, of course,
that they would have till whatever morning time it would
be when the day staff would hit the Sandringham and the
alarm would be raised, but there was no certainty of that.
A late returning or a late arriving patron might have
turned up within minutes after they had pulled out of the
hotel. Even without that, there was Alexandra. Just in the
minutes since we had dropped her she could already have
reached a telephone or why not a police call box? I was
thinking that they would have had some place closer
than New Jersey or Brooklyn where they could have
quickly gone to earth.

Even as I was thinking it, the car pulled up and we
were being herded out of it. We were down one of the
side streets off Lafayette. In all my thinking I had forgotten SoHo. The place where we were stopped was some-
what to the south of the area where the artists had taken
over the old cast-iron loft buildings and converted them
into studios, but it was in a part of town to which the artists were spreading out of that original SoHo nucleus.

Jane and I were hustled out of the car and rushed
across the sidewalk. I had a quick look at the facade of
the building. It was a loft job, but a small one, and it
stood in a street that was as quiet and as dark and as
deserted as the one he had chosen for dumping Alexandra. A few blocks to the north, up in SoHo proper, you
would never find such quiet and such isolation. Up there
it's an area of twenty-four-hour street life.

The inside of the place was a shock. It wasn't just that it was a sculptor's studio, it was that even at first glance I knew where I was. I knew and I couldn't believe it. The night, of course, had been full of surprises, but this was too much. It staggered the imagination.

Does the name, Jack Rabkinski, mean anything to you? It should. Even if sculpture isn't one of your things, or if the sculptors since Rodin's time have lost you, it would still take a bit of doing to escape hearing of Jack Rabkinski. He's been on the cover of *Time*. He's been written up in *Esquire*. In artistic circles his name has long been a household word. But, apart from that, almost any place you live it's not a bad bet that somewhere in your city there's a park or a square or a plaza that has one of Rabkinski's compositions of balanced and counterbalanced girders and that he visited your town to be noisily feted at the unveiling.

I'd never known Rabkinski. I'd never been in his studio. I'd never even known that he had a studio down there in that quiet southern fringe of SoHo, but it made no difference. The moment we came into the place I knew where I was. I had in my time seen far too many Rabkinskis to miss out on recognizing one even at first glance. All over the place there were finished works and works in progress, and every one of them an unmistakable Rabkinski.

More than that, all around the walls there were the sketches, and on a lot of those I had instant recognitions. There was the preliminary sketch for the big Boston piece, a drawing for the one he'd done in Chicago, and a whole set of working drawings for that one that was pictured in all the papers because it had been given as a gift to some city in the Midwest, and there had been a near riot at the installation. Some newspaperman had done a deep-think piece about it and had come up with the great news that it was a constructivist work and that constructivism had begun in Russia. That had done it. They didn't let it go at just hanging Jack Rabkinski in effigy. They hung the effigy from one of the horizontal girders of his sculpture.

I had a good idea of what Rabkinski looked like. I had a clear memory of the occasion when he'd been on the cover of *Time*. So the face we'd seen was not Rabkinski's. I was certain of that. Which of the others he might be I didn't know, but my candidate was the big guy, the one we'd seen only briefly when he was trussing up the hotel people with those leather straps. He was the only one of them who had the size and the muscle, and since he hadn't appeared until the job on the hotel safe had been finished, I could assume that the actual job of the break-in had been in his hands.

In a way it made sense. I knew enough about Rabkinski's working methods to see that. Doing those massive, welded-steel constructions meant replacing the chisel and mallet earlier sculptors used with the welding iron and the acetylene torch. Rabkinski would have all the needed equipment, and he would have the most exquisite expertise in the use of it. If you want a really delicate job done on a safe door, and if you want it done with neatness and finesse, what better safecracker could you find than a sculptor of Jack Rabkinski's type. So it made sense, but wasn't it some mad kind of sense?

Even for a poor, struggling artist it would have hardly seemed possible, but for Jack Rabkinski? Rabkinski had it made. He was the apple of his dealer's eye. He had commissions lined up so far ahead that communities all over the world were waiting their turn to be embellished by a Rabkinski construction. If the man was not already a millionaire, he was well on the way to being one, and without lawbreaking and without risk. The hanging, after all, was never more than in effigy.

Kleptomania? Certainly. It can turn up anywhere and in anyone, but hardly on this scale. Kleptomaniacs are loners. Theirs is the one-man act, sneaky and solitary. They don't pull off any organized, collaborative, carefully planned, and carefully structured larcenies.

I wasn't given much time for looking around, but what time I'd been allowed had been more than enough. I had this one solid, unmistakable fact. Our captors had gone to ground with us in Jack Rabkinski's studio. I tried out the possibility that it might be the place of a Rabkinski collector, but I couldn't work it out for anything like that. There were too many unfinished pieces around, too many works in progress.

So I had my one fact, but I had nothing else I could fit with it. I was allowed only that first quick look around, but I couldn't understand how I could have been permitted even that. True enough, shortly after they'd brought us into the studio they'd blindfolded us, but wasn't that locking the stable door after at least two horses had been stolen? We had seen the face of the man in command and we had seen the studio. We had the two memories fixed in our minds and no blindfold could erase them.

The blindfolds, of course, were preventing our seeing the faces of the other men. They had undoubtedly all skinned out of their nylon-stocking masks. I could understand that. Better that Jane and I should be uncomfortable than that they should be. What I couldn't understand was why it would matter how many faces we might see

now. We had the one man, and we had the place. Just
on that sight of the studio had I not penetrated a second
man's mask, that of the big man with the muscles?

Before the blindfolds had gone on, they'd bound our
arms down at our sides. At first I thought they were going
to truss us up as they had done the men back at the
Sandringham, but they left our feet free. As soon as they
brought out the blindfolds, I understood. Our hands were
fastened only to stop us from tampering with the blindfolds.

Once they had us blindfolded, they separated us. There
again I didn't know what I was to believe about that. The
way the head man put it, there was now nothing for the
two of us to do but wait. Since we had already come close
to losing a full night's sleep, he could think of nothing we
might do with our waiting time that would be better than
catching ourselves some rest. He was all solicitude. He
made it sound as though he were thinking of nothing but
our comfort and well-being. There was a bed for Jane, he
said, but much to his regret there was only the one bed.
That meant I would have to make do with stretching out
on a sofa.

"It's a good sofa, long enough and deep enough, really
outsize. You won't be too uncomfortable on it. Any time
you need the bathroom, just shout. One of the men will
take you. You understand that we can't let you go alone."

"And Miss Harcourt?" I asked.

He sighed.

"Yes," he said, "Miss Harcourt is a problem. All I can
do is try to make it as little discomfiting for her as the circumstances permit. I'll take her myself. At least I won't
be rough with her, and I'll do everything I can to make it
as little embarrassing for her as I can."

"I'm sure she'll think that's a break," I said.

"I wish I could believe that." He made it sound as though he were deeply regretful. "She's a wonderful girl. Under other conditions . . ."

He let it hang there, finishing it only with another sigh.

I had to go. One of the other men took me. Blindfolded as I was, I couldn't be certain which one, but I made a guess that it was the big, burly guy, the one who in my thinking I was now calling Jack Rabkinski. It could have been self-deception. Humiliated by the ease with which the guy pushed me around, I may possibly have preferred to think that I was in the hands of the biggest and the most powerful of them. Much later I did have some verification of my guess.

It would have taken only a small measure of consideration on his part to have made the process less disagreeable. I could accept that they would have considered it necessary that he stand over me and watch me if he had been unbinding my hands, but he left them tied down to my sides while he did for me all the things I couldn't therefore do for myself.

Everything he did, furthermore, he did in a rage, whether it was feeding me a meal or going through the unzipping-and-zipping routine in the john. He said nothing but in mockery, and every touch of his hands he built into a humiliation. I wanted to tell myself that it was nothing more than a perverted sense of humor, but I couldn't convince myself of that. There was too much violent rancor in it. The man smelled of hate.

His hands were big and hard and rough, the hands of a laborer, hands given little or no care. Whenever he put them on me, I felt the rasp of jaggedly broken fingernails.

He fed me coffee and a buttered roll. He enjoyed bang-

ing the rim of the cup against my teeth and splashing
coffee over my chin and down my shirt front. All the
while he kept telling me that I was disgusting. I ate like a
pig. When he left me, there would be someone else to
stand guard over me. They spelled each other at it, but it
was never the head man. Either he had taken off, or he
was busy with other chores, or he was giving himself full-
time to Jane Harcourt. I had no way of knowing which.

Since his was the face we had seen, it could have made
sense for the others to have taken over on the job of holding us while he was making a head start on his getaway.
They could afford delay better than he could. I would get
that far with my thinking, and then inevitably Rabkinski
would pop into my head and I would be asking myself
what Rabkinski could afford. No matter in what direction
I tried to cast my line of thought, it came back to that.
How could Jack Rabkinski afford to let either Jane or me
remain alive?

By considering other possibilities I tried to sheer
away from any answer to that question. The head man
could be occupied with other chores. Surely there would
be things that would need doing. Dividing the loot?
Fencing the loot? Stowing it away for later disposal? And
certainly the remaining possibility was equally reasonable. The man had been attracted to Jane. He'd shown that
clearly enough. Certainly they would consider it as necessary to keep her under constant guard as they did me.

I could well imagine that he would be unwilling to
trust any of the others alone with her. It seemed inevitable that he had reserved that duty for himself. My attend-
ant had just poured the coffee into and over me, and he'd
just had me to the john. I was fresh from all that and
stretched out on the sofa, and I was trying to visualize

how those same offices had been performed for her. Had
he found a way that would stop somewhere this side of
rape, or was he going for broke?

I kept telling myself that I couldn't sleep, I had to
think. I had to be prepared. I was going to have to find
some way of dealing with it when it came. That in itself
might have been too big an order. To have been prepared
to meet it, when I didn't even have a clue to what it was
going to be, was an impossibility.

Despite my determination to stay awake, I drifted off
into sleep. It had been creeping up on twenty-four hours
since I'd last been to bed. Exhaustion took over. There
was also the blindfold. Under it my eyes were held shut.
Try it sometime. Go without sleep nearly all the way
around the clock and then shut your eyes with every in-
tention of popping them open again and staying awake.
You'll see what happens. You'll cork off.

It was by no means the best kind of sleep, hardly the
deep and dreamless restorative variety. I had all manner
of dreams. Alexandra was in one of them. She was being
mugged, and it was one of the parsnip heads doing it. It
was the big guy and he had the leather straps. He was
garroting Alexandra with one of them.

I was there and I was trying to get to her. It seemed to
me that I was running hard, but I could have been running on a treadmill: I was coming no closer. Maybe I
woke from that dream and drifted right off again to have
another. I know only that I went into another dream. This
one had me in Spain—back in the Inquisition. There was a
procession of the condemned being driven to the stake.
You know those pointed hats they were forced to wear?

They were wearing them, but then the hats turned into
nylon-stocking masks, and the condemned were all blob-

heads with the point on top. At the beginning I was just a spectator, but by one of those dream-stuff transitions that takes you from here to there without any rational path between, I became one of the condemned. I was no longer watching the procession. I was in it with the stocking forced down over my head. I was trying to tear it away, but Rabkinski had hold of my hands and he wouldn't let me get at it.

Then the procession came to a halt, but it wasn't at the stake. It was a scaffold instead, except that this scaffold was a Rabkinski assemblage. I was trying to decide whether it was the one he'd done for Chicago or the Boston one. It didn't look quite like either of those two, and I was telling myself that it was difficult to know because all those people it had hanging from it confused the form. The people were all wearing the stocking masks and they were all hanging from the girders. They were hanging by the neck.

Coming awake from that one, I was soaking wet. I sat up. There was nothing I could have wanted more than to be able to wipe the sweat away from my face and neck; but, with my arms tied down the way they were, there was nothing I could do about it. I couldn't even begin to guess how long I might have slept. I asked for the time.

"You ain't going nowhere."

I knew the voice. This was the lug who'd stood guard on us while we'd been waiting in the bar at the Sandringham. It had been one of the others before I fell asleep. This was the first I knew that they were taking the duty in shifts. I took it to mean that I had been asleep for some considerable time. I set myself to try to work out some idea of what they might be doing. My first thought was that, using us as hostages, they were trying to make a deal by which they would swap us for a safe getaway. I couldn't work that out for anything that even the stupidest crooks would attempt.

They had opened themselves up too much, and they had done it needlessly. The head man had shown his face. I could understand that. There had been no help for it. He had been trapped by his allergy. Until he had been at close quarters with us in the car, he'd had no idea of what Alexandra's perfume would do to him.

The reaction of the others had been simple enough. I couldn't like it, but I could understand it. Once he had ripped off the nylon and we had seen his face, he was in danger, and from him the danger could rub off on the rest of the gang. We had become witnesses who could identify him. There could be only one sure way out of that for them. The three of us had to be eliminated, none of us left alive to hand the police a description or to make an identification. They had been ready for it. I had the feeling that they had been eager for it.

But there was the head man. Since it was his face we had seen, he was the one who was most in jeopardy, but he was also the one who had jibbed at murder. He'd let Alexandra go. I was having some trouble understanding that, but I could like it. Certainly I could read it as giving Jane and me a new lease on life. The difference between one witness and three would be negligible. Anything we might add to what she would tell the police—to what she was almost certainly already telling the police—would make little or no difference. Nothing could be gained from eliminating us now, and they had everything to lose. If they should be caught, they already had enough crimes charged against them. To add murder would be insane.

There was encouragement in that thinking, but I had to

tell myself that there was no certainty. Except for the one man, they were an ugly bunch. If the thing started to go sour for them, there would be no telling what they might do. It wouldn't have to make sense. It wouldn't have to be to their advantage. They could act stupidly and insanely to no purpose at all, just out of rage and frustration. They had the two of us in their hands. If they saw things turning against them, they might take it out on us.

What was most worrying was the insanity of the thing. In any kidnapping I'd ever heard of, unless the victim was a small infant, there would be every effort made to keep the victims ignorant of where they were taken. If they were ever to be released, it would have to be with no knowledge of where they had been held, no possibility of leading the police to the place. In our case it had been handled as though they were planning to kill us. They weren't in the least concerned about our knowing that we were in the Rabkinski studio. Trying to line it up from Rabkinski's point of view, I was face to face with total madness.

The man's a sculptor. He has it made as only a very few people in the arts ever get it made. He has a worldwide reputation. The money is pouring in. How does he get himself involved in a robbery, and why would he? The man would have to be insane, and that isn't all of it. They bring us to his studio.

Okay. They don't expect that I'll recognize the work as Rabkinski's, although that's a silly expectation for work that's had so much publicity. There's also the matter of the artist's vanity. Could Jack Rabkinski be so modest that he would think that anyone could see his work and fail to recognize it as something from his master hand? So far as I could remember, nobody had ever accused Jack Rabkinski of modesty.

Anyhow, it didn't matter that I'd seen the sculptures and the sketches. Jane and I had seen the street, and we had seen the building. I knew precisely where it was. I could lead the police straight to it, and that would be all it would take. I didn't need to know whose studio it was. Once I'd led them to it, they'd find out quickly enough.

Try to make sense of that. Let's say the loot was phenomenal. Cash wouldn't be the biggest part of it. The major fortune would be in jewelry, and a fortune like that shrinks mightily when the stuff has to be fenced. Everybody knows that much. So Rabkinski, if all goes well—and that's a big if—will be in line to pull down one-sixth of it. How much can that come to? The equivalent of what he gets out of one sculpture commission or even out of ten?

For that is he going to give up everything? He'll have to disappear. He can never surface again. He's finished himself as an artist, and where can he go to hide? He's not a Mr. Nobody who can skip the country, take on a new identity, and hope that he can find some part of the world where he can live without being recognized. Is there any place on earth where he can go? The jungles of New Guinea? Does he need the loot for that? What can he do with money in the wilds of New Guinea?

Obviously, there's no profit in killing us just because we'd seen the one face, not with Alexandra out there alive to tell what she'd seen. But now we've been permitted to see the studio. Are we to be killed to stop our telling about that? If I am right about the big husky one being Rabkinski, I can't deceive myself about him. On this, our having seen his studio, it's his neck that's first on the line,

and I can't think it will bother him the first bit to knock
the two of us off.

I'd gone only that far when he took over.

"I've got lunch for you," he said.

That was something, at least. It wasn't the exact time,
but I could infer noon or some time thereabouts.

"Do you want me to put you on the potty before you
eat or after? . . . Sure you can wait? Nobody around
here's going to change your diaper."

"I can wait."

Without telling me it was coming, he shoved something
at my face. Only some of it got into my mouth; the rest of
it hit my lap. I think it was some kind of a sandwich. You
lose a lot from your recognition of food when you can't
see it or hold it in your hand. If he had told me when he
was pushing it at me and given me time to open up and
take a bite, I might have had some better idea of it; but
he was playing games.

He'd say nothing. He'd just ram it against my mouth,
and he would make sure that I couldn't work out his
rhythm. He came at me with it at irregular intervals. All I
could do was open my mouth quickly as soon as I felt him
punch it into my face. I'd get some sort of a bite out of it
before he pulled it away. He followed it with coffee,
which he poured impartially into me and onto me.

Taking me to the john was a repeat on his earlier performance. He fancied himself as a comedian. I would
have been happy to think it was no more than that. I
couldn't. There was too much malice in it.

So then it was back to the sofa and back to silence and
waiting. I took up where I had left off with my thinking. I
had come to the place where it seemed to me that Jack
Rabkinski had good reason for knocking off the two of us.

It would make no difference to him that Alexandra was out there talking her head off. She hadn't seen the studio. They had dropped her in quite another part of town.

That much was simple enough. The rest, however, was ridiculously gratuitous. Why had we been permitted to see the street or the building, much less catch even a glimpse of the inside of the studio? Couldn't we have been blindfolded in the car?

It seemed insane that they should have handled the thing in a way that so severely limited their options. Bringing us to the studio the way they did, I began to think, could only have been acting on a death wish. The deaths, however, were going to be Jane's and mine. Could they be that crazy? That hungry to do murder? If that was it, why did they go to these ridiculous lengths to give themselves a reason? Couldn't they have just done it without a reason?

If they had to bring us here, they could so easily have blindfolded us before we were anywhere near here, but they had waited until it was just too late. So why were we blindfolded now? When I'd started on this thinking, I'd thought I knew the reason for that. It had seemed simple enough, but, of course, it wasn't.

I'd had that all taped out. They wanted to be out of the nylon-stocking masks. If someone had to be uncomfortable, better we than they. So what's wrong with that? It doesn't fit with the rest of it. If we're not permitted to stay alive to tell about the studio, what would it matter if we saw their faces? We weren't going to be alive to identify them.

Your head fills up with these questions and answers. Every logical line dead-ends at another line that is contradictory but equally logical. You work at pulling all these

disparate lines together into some single reasonable se-
quence, and all you get for your efforts is the feeling that
you don't have a head on you, you have a squirrel cage;
where your mind should be, you have a treadmill.

I was thinking and thinking and I wore myself out with
it. Sometime during what I presumed to be an intermina-
ble afternoon I dropped off to sleep again. This time I
was wakened. A lusty backhander to the side of my head
brought me up out of sleep. I came up with my ears
ringing.

It was supper time and the same thing all over again. It
was the same suggestion made in the same way. He had
no oversupply of such excruciatingly funny lines, or
maybe he was especially enamored of that one. The
feeding was the same. I can describe it only as assault by
sandwich and coffee.

Nobody was telling me the time. I had only the meal
schedule to go by. I was calling it evening. It had been a
long day, and as time went on, it was stretching into a
longer night. I was past thinking. The more I worked at
it, the farther I seemed to be from any conclusion other
than that we'd fallen afoul of a band of lunatics, and it
was no good trying to guess what could be going on in
their heads.

I suppose I'd have been ready to settle for that much
earlier, if it hadn't been that each time I came to that
same dead end, there popped into my head memories of
many talks I'd had with my friend, Inspector Schmidt.

"Saying that they're crazy," he would tell me, "is no
answer. It's only the easy out in any case that isn't open
and shut. It's always a possibility. Of course, it is. Nobody's saying there's no such thing as the criminally insane, but it's no good using it as an escape hatch. There's

a reason for what they're doing. It may not be a good reason, but it seems good to them. It has its own kind of logic. The job is to find your way into that logic."

I couldn't argue with the memory. I knew well enough that it was the job. I could only wish that I could get the inspector out of my head and into that studio. The wish, of course, was futile. Jane Harcourt and I were on our own.

I may have slept some during that night. I don't think I did. What with some morning sleep and a long afternoon sleep, I was slept out. I was thought out too, but my mental treadmill kept going. It was taking me nowhere. Time had stretched so long that, when suddenly I heard the man's voice, I thought it would be morning again. It was the first he'd been near me all day and all night. That is, if he had come into the studio where they were holding me at any point during that time, I hadn't been aware of it. He hadn't spoken.

Now he was speaking but not to me.

"I'll take over on him," he said. "It's pulling out time. All the others are out already and on their way, only us left. So now you take off. I'll finish up here."

There was no answer, just a click of metal on metal. The man laughed.

"I unloaded it while you were sleeping," he said. "I'm the only one who never slept. Mine's the only one still loaded."

A string of clicks and a string of curses. The man broke in on them.

"All the others were sensible and went quietly," he said. "They were disappointed as you are, but they decided that they wanted to live. It's your choice now. You go quietly and you're all right. Try anything, and I'm ready to kill you. I'll try to put it where you'll die quickly, even though I doubt that you were going to do that much for me."

"Look."

"I have looked and I saw," the man said. "Each of you in turn—each one's made his try. I knew you would. Once I let Mrs. Gordon go, it had to be. I was a liability. I'm still a liability. If you're smart, you'll get away from me as quick as you can. Move."

I heard them go. I gambled that they were going together. Just on hearing alone I tried to place the way they were going. I was alone and I could move. I would be doing it blind and without the use of my hands, but there was nothing wrong with my legs. If I could move and quickly, could I find some way out of the place before he would be back to "finish up here"?

I wanted a window. They'd never taken me upstairs. I was down at street level. If I could find a window and kick the glass out, then maybe, just maybe.

I was trying to feel my way, but that studio was no place for going it blind. It was inevitable. I fell afoul of one of the Rabkinski constructions. The steel took me at ankle height and I went sprawling. Tangled in that complex assemblage of girders and unable to grab at anything with my hands, I was having trouble getting back to my feet.

Hands took hold of me and helped me up.

"Mr. Bagby," the man said, "so far you've not been difficult. Now is no time to begin."

III

"Maybe a man's got to begin sometime," I said.

I liked the idea even though I knew I was in no position for it. I was on my feet. If I could believe what I'd heard, I was in a one-on-one situation. It was just me and the man. The others presumably had taken off. Since in the process of setting me back on my feet he had both his hands on me, I knew that for those moments at least he didn't have his gun at the ready. For one imbecilic moment I had the thought of making a grab at it. My hands strained against the strap that was holding them secured to my sides. They were in there on their own trying for the grab. I had to remind them of their futility and tell them to relax.

They could do nothing. In fact, without my eyes to guide them, they could do less than nothing. I seemed to be surrounded by steel. I was standing in a sculptural maze. It seemed to me that any way I moved I would be tripping myself up again. The man's hands came away from me, and when he next spoke it was from a distance. It was impossible to estimate how far he had withdrawn.

"In a little while," he said, "it will be your time to begin, Mr. Bagby, but first you must be very careful. You

must listen closely. You must have an exact understanding of what I say to you. You must be careful to follow my instructions to the letter. Miss Harcourt's safety
and your own will depend on it. You must take my word
for it that we are in this together now, the three of
us—Miss Harcourt, you, and I. We have been ever since I
allowed Mrs. Gordon to go off alive. From that moment
my good friends were convinced that their safety required three killings—yours, Miss Harcourt's, and mine.
Mrs. Gordon had seen my face, and Mrs. Gordon was
away and alive. She can identify me, and they are afraid
that through me they will be identified as well. Surely you
can understand their reasoning."

"*Their* reasoning, yes," I said, "but what about yours?
You let Mrs. Gordon go. What good can you do yourself
by killing us?"

"None, and that's only one of the reasons why I don't
want to kill you. But you must help me. I have all the
others disarmed and out of the way. They may be having
ideas of rearming and coming back here. Give them
enough time and they can do it. They could be waiting
outside to shoot us down as we come out, but not until
they have been somewhere first to rearm. So that's the
time we have."

"We?"

"Yes, Mr. Bagby, the three of us. Standing just where
you are now and moving only in place, start turning very
slowly to the right. Very slowly, so that I can tell you at
the exact moment when to stop. Everything depends on
your co-operation, on your most precise obedience to my
instructions. Without that we might use up too much
time, and then we'll all three be dead. Start turning."

I could make no sense of what he was telling me, but I

could do no better than take him at his word. He was
there. I couldn't see him, but he could see me. He had the
use of his hands, and I didn't. He was almost certainly
holding his gun on me. If nothing else, it seemed as
though I had no better choice than to humor him.

Moving in place, I turned slowly to the right.

"Stop," he said.

I stopped.

"Listen before you move again," he said. "If you move
as I tell you to and take not even the smallest step in any
other direction, you will be free of that sculpture you tangled with. I will be moving you out into the open and
shifting you to the spot where you have to be. Be guided
by my voice. I will keep talking. Walk straight toward my
voice, but slowly. The time will come when I will tell you
to change direction, and the time will come when I will
tell you to stop. We haven't time for any mistakes."

He moved me straight forward for about five paces and
then he put me through a ninety-degree turn to the right.
Then for what seemed a very long walk he guided me in a
straight line. On my memory of what I'd seen of that vast
studio before I was blindfolded, I was guessing that he
was moving me over most of the length of it. Finally he
told me to stop.

"I know it's difficult since you can't use your hands, but
do the best you can. I want you down on your knees."

A picture flashed into my mind and my every muscle
tensed. You know the picture. Chinese executions—the
blindfolded victim with his arms bound to his sides waits
kneeling for the bullet in the back of his head. It was
becoming almost impossible to believe that this would not
be a madman's sadistic game. I was even thinking that
the calm and the logic of the man's performance were of

themselves insane. Wasn't it crazy for him to be so coolly rational about all this?

"If you move your left hand a little, and you can move it that much," he said, "you'll hit a bar you can grab hold of. Holding on to that, you'll have less trouble getting down."

I reached the few inches I could manage with my wrist bound tight down to my side. The back of my hand came up against the bar. I got my fingers around it.

"And what's the kneeling for?" I asked. "You want me to beg?"

"I need to have you sitting on the floor," he said. "I'm trying to get you down there without your injuring yourself. Please, trust me. I have this all worked out. I'm doing it the way that will be best for the three of us."

Following his step-by-step instructions, I lowered myself first to my knees and then worked myself around to where I was sitting on the floor the way he wanted me.

"Good," he said. "We're almost through. There is only this next bit, and while we're doing it you will have an opportunity to be difficult. I must ask you not to take it because it can do no good. You will only force me to knock you out, and I don't want to do that. This will go much better for Miss Harcourt and you if I don't have to knock you out. It will make things no worse for me, but I'd like it to be as easy as possible for the three of us. I have another strap like the one that's binding your arms. I have to put it around your ankles. It will be all right. Just trust me."

"Do I have a choice?" I asked.

"A limited choice," he replied. "It is whether you will force me to pistol whip you or not."

"Since you seem to find that distasteful," I said, "I wouldn't think of forcing you."

"Good man."

He sounded a lot nearer. He was moving in on me and talking all the way. He told me why he kept talking. He wanted me to have the best possible idea of where he was. He wanted me to know when he would be close enough to take hold of my ankles.

"I know that, doing this the way I am, I'm letting you know just when you can most effectively kick out at me. I'm trusting you not to do that. I'm trusting you to believe me when I say it can serve no purpose but to impede me in my efforts to act for our joint benefit."

I had to trust him. After all, he'd laid it on the line. I could submit and remain conscious. I could give myself the satisfaction of trying to land a good kick and pay for it with his gun butt knocking me on the head.

He was quick and he was efficient. As soon as he had the strap fastened around my ankles, he backed away from me. I could estimate where he was by his voice.

"So far so good," he said. "Now, I'm going to get Miss Harcourt and bring her down here. I won't be long."

It seemed to me that he was gone for the better part of forever. I began wondering whether he would be coming back at all. I kept telling myself that a man's sense of time would be seriously awry in a situation like mine. It was probably not nearly as long as I thought. Just sitting there bound head and foot was getting to me. I experimented with moving. I could slide myself along but only inches at a time. Drawing up my knees and digging in my heels while I simultaneously pushed with my hands against the floor, I could move myself forward just that tiny distance. It was only an inch or two, but the inches could be built

into feet and the feet into yards. I wasn't letting myself
look ahead to anything as practical as a question of where
it could get me. It was something to do. Whether it
served any purpose or not, I had to do something. Such
was my state of mind.

So I sweated out my few inches and added to them the
next few inches. I'd moved forward perhaps as much as a
foot when I was stopped cold. I had come up against a
wall. I was about to try it the other way, pushing backward, when the man returned.

"Oh, come now, Mr. Bagby," he said. "I had you posi-
tioned to your best advantage. You must recognize that I
can see and you can't. Trust me, please, to know better
than you precisely where you should be."

Again it was the painstakingly exact instructions, the
few inches this way and the few inches that to put me on
just the one spot he had chosen for me. When he was
satisfied with my placement, he told me to stop and stay
where I was without moving. He switched away from me
and began talking to Jane. I could judge only by the
sound of their voices. It seemed to me that the sound was
coming to me over a considerable distance. I guessed that
it would be the full length of Rabkinski's vast studio
space.

From what they were saying I could gather that he was
doing with her much as he had done with me, getting her
down on the floor, positioning her exactly, binding her ankles. There was, however, a difference. With her he
seemed to have full confidence in her co-operation. I
couldn't say that he had been rough with me. The others
at every opportunity had been—and most particularly the
one I'd tabbed as Rabkinski—but this guy had always
been considerate. Even when he had been threatening,

the threats had been gently made. The difference was
that in talking to her he was doing it without even the
faintest suggestion of threat.

With her, therefore, it went quickly. Then there was a
moment of silence and, when he spoke again, it was from
a recognizably shorter distance.

"Now," he said, "I have you exactly where you should
be."

My mind read that for his having us exactly where he
wanted us, but with an effort I put such thinking aside. I
had to strip my mind of everything but concentration on
what he was saying to us.

"Speak to each other," he said.

"Are you all right, Miss Harcourt?" I asked.

"I am, Mr. Bagby," she said. "And you?"

"All right," I said, "but call me George."

"If you will call me Jane."

The man broke in on us.

"Good," he said. "I'm going to leave you now. If Jane
keeps talking, George can guide himself on her voice and
slide himself across the floor toward her. From where he
is now, if he works himself toward Jane's voice, he will
have a completely clear path across the studio—no obstacles, no problems. It will be slow work, but in time the
two of you will come together. I'm sorry I have to make it
so difficult, but you will understand that it is the time I
need for getting myself well away from here. Once you
have come together you'll be all right. One of you can
free the other's hands and, once one of you has free
hands, it will be no time at all before both of you will be
completely freed. With your blindfolds off, you will see
the phone. You will, of course, phone the police. I can't
expect that you'll do otherwise. I wish all this could have

been different and that I could have come to know you better, the both of you. I like you and I admire you. But this is it. I'm saying good-by. Can you wish me luck?"

"I can," Jane said. "I do."

In my heart I could as well, but I wasn't saying it. I stayed very still and listened. I heard the sound of a shutting door.

"He's gone," I said. "If you will talk to me and keep talking, I'll work my way across to you as quickly as I can."

"Poor man," she said. "I know I shouldn't be wanting him to get away, but I can't help it. I do want it and with all my heart. He's so sweet and kind and good, and we do owe him. We owe him everything. He's saved our lives. If it weren't for him, we'd both be dead. Those others, they wanted to kill us, and they would have done it without turning a hair. Of course, they would have killed him too. He was saving his own life along with ours, but that was only because he'd already saved Mrs. Gordon's life. If he had let them shoot her, then he would have been safe and it would have been only our lives, but he couldn't do that. He couldn't because he's a good man. He's good and he's kind and he's gentle."

I was thinking that what she was saying was true enough as far as it went, but it didn't go all the way. I was remembering that at the very first it had been he who had said he had plans for Alexandra and me. The idea of taking us along as hostages had been his. I could believe that he had planned it in the conviction that he could bring it off without doing us any harm. He hadn't foreseen the bad luck of Alexandra's perfume and his allergy, but nevertheless, it had been his idea that had put us in jeopardy.

That, furthermore, was not all of it. There was the studio. I was thinking that bringing us to the studio had been an insanity. The police would be going after Rabkinski. There was that weakness in the gang's setup. In the light of that, did it matter much that one man's face had been seen by the three of us. They were sticking themselves with the fatal weakness of the studio. That should be more than enough. This second weakness wouldn't matter much.

I was thinking all this but I was saying nothing. I was saving my breath for the laborious job of sliding myself backward across the studio floor, targeting myself on the sound of her voice. I was moving along, but it was exhausting work. Past the sound of her own voice, she heard me pant.

"George," she said. "Let's take turns. Rest awhile and talk to me. I'll try working myself toward your voice."

"I'm all right," I said. "I can do it."

"I didn't say you couldn't, but it will be quicker if we take turns. I'm fresh and you aren't. If you rest awhile and let me take over, you can come back to it refreshed and you'll do better."

"Do you want it to be quicker?" I asked. "You want him to get away. The more time he has . . ."

"He's taken care of that, George. He's given himself a good head start."

"All the time we've been here," I said, "it's been the others guarding me, bringing me food, pushing it into my mouth, taking me to the john. He never came near me until now at the last."

"I know," she said. "He was doing everything for me.

None of the others came near me. I suppose he wouldn't let them."

"And he did nothing to make it rough on you?"

"He couldn't have been kinder or more considerate or more decent."

"The john?"

She didn't answer that.

"Keep talking, George. I need my breath for moving myself along, and I have to hear you to guide on you."

"The big muscle man took me, and he worked at making it ugly and humiliating. It would have been bad enough in any case, but he worked at making it nasty."

"Keep talking, George."

I was getting no answers, even though I was telling myself that it was none of my damn business. If she had been so pleased with the way the man had treated her, who was I to be questioning her? It wasn't impossible that she liked the way he had handled her. You can be thinking that I have a dirty mind, but I'm a writer and trying to learn how people tick is a big part of a writer's job.

Her last "Keep talking, George," had had a hint of breathlessness in it. It could have been emotional—her reaction to the question that was implicit in what I was saying. I chose to read it as a signal that the time had come for me to take over from her.

"Your turn to talk," I said. "I'm rested and you're wearing yourself out."

I was curious to know what she would talk about. I was masking my curiosity behind solicitude. She talked, but I was left with my curiosity. She wasn't telling me anything. She speculated on how Alexandra had done. She worked up a lot of concern about that. Alexandra, after all, would have had a long walk before she could have come to anything that would take her off the dark and lonely streets down in that warehouse neighborhood.

She'd been worrying about Alexandra and she was still worried. Alexandra, she said, wasn't a young woman. We'd been all right because the head man was good and kind and gentle. Whatever angle she took in her talk, she was always drawn back to that. It seemed to be sitting at the center of her mind and acting like a magnet for all her thinking.

Alexandra, however, had been turned loose to deal with whatever might have come her way. Might she not have been mugged? Might she not have been killed? Had she done that long walk unmolested? Had she reached safety? At her age under stress, might she not have had a heart attack or a stroke along those dark, deserted streets?

"Alexandra is tougher than you think," I said. "All the time she was with us she was going through the whole thing without the first symptom of stress. She might even have been enjoying herself. I know Alexandra."

I was thinking that I didn't know Jane, but I was not at all certain that she hadn't been enjoying herself. Jane took my interruption to mean that I had again tired and that again I was to talk while she took over. I had to insist on going on.

"I've got the knack of it now," I said. "I'm moving in on you fast. I can tell from listening to you. Keep talking. I won't say anything."

She talked. I don't remember much of what she said. She was just repeating and rephrasing what she had already said. I listened only to the extent that I was guiding myself on the sound of her voice. I was totally concentrated on pulling myself along across that endless floor.

I finally made it but not before I'd taken to wondering whether I would have any seat left in my pants. It was a form of locomotion that was taking the skin off the heels of my hands, and they weren't being nearly as heavily abraded as my butt. We came together back to back.

I turned myself a quarter circle, feeling along the belt that bound her arms until my fingers touched the buckle. Everything was working out exactly as the man had said it would. Loosening the strap was only a moment's work.

"Thanks," she said. "My hands are free. Can you turn now so I can reach the buckle on yours?"

"Work on yourself first," I told her. "Take off your blindfold and free your ankles. Then you can turn me loose. It will be quicker that way."

"Yes," she said, "I suppose so. To be honest with you, George, I don't know that I want it to be quicker. I want him to have all the time in the world. I want him to get away."

"I want to get out of here."

"I know. We must get out of here. There are the others. How do we know that with him gone they won't be coming back? I'll be with you in a moment. I have my blindfold off. I'll have my legs done in a second."

"Take your time," I said. "A minute one way or the other won't matter."

"Every minute can matter to him," she said. "You should have had me turn you loose first, George. You shouldn't have tempted me."

"Tempted you?"

"Yes. As soon as I have you free, you'll be calling the police. I could leave you as you are, and I could just go off. I could give him a couple of hours and then call the police and tell them where to find you."

"Oh, come on," I said.

"I know. I can't do that even if I want to. I can't leave you here because they may come back."

I didn't expect that any of them would be coming back, but on that point I was holding my tongue. In this debate she was having with herself there was only that one fear to pull in my favor. She did have me sweating a bit, though, until I felt her hands on the strap buckle. She was freeing my arms. As soon as I had the use of them, I began working on my blindfold. Despite what she'd been saying about wanting to win every last minute for the man, she played fair with me. Even while I was grappling with my blindfold, she was down at my ankles freeing my legs.

There were no lights on in the studio, but it was only half dark. The windows were showing the first gray of dawn. There was something strange about the windows. I was remembering the studio as it had been in the few moments before we were blindfolded. I had noticed something about the windows then and was now trying to remember. I pulled my mind away from the effort, telling myself that it couldn't be important. I turned my back on the windows to look for the telephone. At that moment Jane switched on the lights. Only just out from behind the blindfold, my eyes were dazzled. For a couple of moments the glare had me blinded again. I could see nothing.

Blinking myself back to sight, I saw Jane. She was taking stuff out of her coat pocket—a compact and a comb. She looked at herself in the mirror of the compact. She was giggling. She was a strange and even comic sight. Her hair was flattened and matted where the blindfold had pressed it tight against her skull. Her eyes were a strangely smeared mess. It took me a moment to figure that out, but of course, it was the blindfold again. Her mascara had been rubbed off her lashes and on to her lids. Her eye shadow, evidently in exchange, had been transferred from lids to lashes. The effect might have been less startling if her lips hadn't been freshly anointed with lipstick, perfectly applied, and if her nose and cheeks and chin weren't delicately matt with a light dusting of face powder, also freshly and perfectly applied.

"He did his best," she said. "Of course, he couldn't do my eyes."

She was bringing out of her pockets all her paraphernalia: tissues, eye shadow, mascara, a couple of little brushes. She went to work on her eye make-up.

I spotted the phone. It was clear across the studio. I started for it.

"He put lipstick on you and powdered your nose?" I asked.

"And beautifully too," she said. "George, you must admit he's sweet."

"I suppose he is," I conceded. "He's out of his head, but he's a sweet nut. Sweet, larcenous, and quite mad."

I was about to pick up the phone.

"George," she said. "Don't, please, don't."

"Don't what?"

"Don't call the police. Not from here. Just give me a sec to fix my face and run a comb through my hair, and we'll get out of here. We'll go somewhere else to phone."

"Why?"

"We have to get out of here. I don't want to wait for them to come back."

"While you're fixing your face and running the comb

through your hair, I can dial 911. I'll be through on the phone before you can possibly be ready."

"But then we'll have to stay here, waiting for the police to come."

"So?"

"They might get back before the police come. I want to get out of here."

I picked up the phone and dialed.

"You can go if you like. I'll wait for the police."

She caught her breath. It was almost a sob.

"Out there alone? Suppose they're out there waiting to get me when I come out?"

"Then they're out there waiting to get the two of us when we come out. What good could I do you?"

"You're being unkind," she said.

I didn't answer that. I was through to the police and I had zeroed in on what was bothering me about the windows. There were heavy draperies, and when they had first brought us into the studio, in those few moments before they blindfolded us, I had seen no windows. The draperies had been drawn across them, blanking them out. Now the draperies were pulled back. The windows were showing the growing daylight.

All I had to do was identify myself, tell them we were both alive and well, and fill them in on where we were. I couldn't give them the house number, but I had the street location and I could tell them it was the Rabkinski studio.

"Don't anyone bother to look the number up," I said. "Just come into the street. We'll come out when we hear your sirens."

I hung up and turned back to Jane.

"They knew about us," I said. "Alexandra wasn't mugged and she wasn't killed. She's been working with the police. She got to them with the first news of the robbery."

"I suppose she's described him."

I've never seen a woman look more woebegone.

"I suppose."

"And you'll give them your description as well."

"Won't you?"

"I don't remember what he looked like. I never got a really good look. I couldn't possibly identify him."

She might have been rehearsing the way she would do it for the police. She didn't need the rehearsal. She was handing me a masterful performance.

"Oh, Jane, come on now."

"I know it will do no good with Alexandra and you telling them," she said, "but I can't help it. I just can't make myself do anything that might hurt him."

"Now look, Jane. They pulled off the silliest, most insane caper in the history of crime. If the police don't break this through our recognizing your sweet, gentle, kind friend . . ."

She didn't wait for me to finish. She broke in on me.

"He is," she said. "He's all of that and a lot more."

"Sure, and that lot more is insanity. I was about to say the police are bound to break this no matter what. They'll break it through Rabkinski."

"Who's Rabkinski?"

"The big, mean one with the muscles."

"None of us saw his face."

"We're right here in his studio. We're surrounded by his sculptures. He cut the hotel safe-deposit boxes open. He did it with his acetylene torch and his other equipment. He's an expert in the handling of that stuff. He's always cutting heavy steel to make these sculptures. Okay.

They're all of them off and gone by now. Your sweet, kind, gentle friend did a great job of fixing that. Maybe he can disappear. Maybe the others can disappear. But Rabkinski? He's world famous. There's no place he can go where he won't be known. He'll have no place to hide."

She looked around at the constructions. It could have been that she was seeing them for the first time.

"This stuff?" she said. "World famous? Now *you're* crazy."

I was about to tell her to wait and see, but I heard the sirens. I went to open the doors to the police instead.

The street was filling with police cars. The number didn't surprise me. A robbery of such dimensions capped with a kidnapping, that's major crime and the NYPD responds to major crimes.

Nevertheless, I spotted one car out there that I hadn't expected. At the sight of it I went cold. I knew that car. I'd ridden in it more times than I could count. There was no reason why it should have been there. Inspector Schmidt is Chief of Homicide and there had been no death. There had been the robbery and the kidnapping, but there had been no murder. This wasn't the inspector's department, or was it?

Alexandra? Over the phone they'd said she was all right, but that might have been to spare me the shock until they could break it to me face to face.

The man? If his partners had been able to come up with fresh armament during the time he was setting up Jane and me, they could have gotten to him. They would have been gunning for him if they could, and although it seemed too quick, it might not have been. But for the police to know about it already and, more than that, to have it connected to Jane and me, that was much too quick. It could only have been done if Alexandra had viewed the body and had identified the man as one of our kidnappers. There hadn't been nearly enough time for all of that. It wasn't possible.

So again Alexandra, and they hadn't wanted to tell me on the phone.

Schmitty came leaping out of his car. Within a moment his hands were all over me. I guess seeing me wasn't enough. He was making certain that all of me was intact. I was complete and undamaged.

"You okay, Baggy?" he said.

"Not a bit the worse for wear," I told him. I saw no reason for going into details like the heels of my hands and the seat of my pants. "What are you doing here?" I asked. "Tell me. Who?"

"Who what?"

"Who was killed?"

Schmitty grinned.

"Nobody was killed," he said.

"Then what are you doing here?"

"Just calling on a friend, you dope. You ought to know you're my friend. Didn't that Mrs. Gordon tell you so? She told everybody else. It's the only thing that got you kidnapped. She made that clear enough. Being my friend. So I'm responsible."

With a carefully modulated backhander to the side of my head, he rocked me.

"What am I doing here? he asks."

IV

I told the police everything I knew, and it was evident that for the earlier part of it they'd already had a complete and competent report from Alexandra and the hotel people. Jane was adding nothing much. It was obvious that she was working hard at knowing as little as possible. Aware that there was a glaring discrepancy between what she was offering and what the detectives were having from Alexandra and me, she put on a big act of shock and distress. Suddenly she was a flitterwitted, hysterical female who couldn't trust herself to be remembering anything right.

The face we had seen? She insisted that she'd never caught a good look at it. She was certain that she would never know the man if she were to see him again. She proclaimed herself equally incompetent on sizes and shapes and voices. She apologized for her inability to be more helpful, but certainly they wouldn't want her to tell them anything of which she was less than certain.

There was only the one area in which she had anything competent to offer, and there she was not merely offering. She was pushing hard. The leader of the gang had treated us with every consideration. He had, at the risk of his own life, saved ours. She hoped that would always be remembered in extenuation of what he'd done. She, for one, would never forget it.

So there was the one point on which the three of us were unanimous. I must confess, in fact, that there was one detail on which even Alexandra and I held back. I said nothing to indicate that the kidnapping had evidently been the head man's idea, and the first time I had a moment alone with Alexandra, I learned that she had been similarly reticent on that one point.

"The poor lad," she said. "Maybe it's because I'm a woman, George, or even because I was a woman once . . ."

I broke in on her to take issue with that "once."

"Sweet of you to say so, darling, at my age," she resumed. "Anyhow I can understand Jane's feelings. He is a charmer, and he was performing so well. You must admire a smooth and expert performance even if it is criminal, mustn't you? It was just bad luck, the poor lamb—my perfume and his allergy and that close, unventilated car. You do say it yourself. He was extraordinarily kind to us and beautifully polite, and we do owe him our lives."

"Agreed, agreed," I said, "but smooth as he was, he wasn't all that expert. He was incredibly stupid. I grant you that he couldn't have foreseen the problem with your perfume, but even without that he was blowing it. Taking Jane and me to that studio, letting us see where we were, and leaving us there to call the police—that was idiotic. Maybe the police will catch up with him, and the two of us will identify him. Jane won't. She's determined not to."

"I hope they won't catch up with him," Alexandra said. "I know it's wrong of me, but I'm going to hate having to testify against the poor boy. I'll do it, of course. One has no choice, but I shall hate it."

"If the police do catch up with him," I said, "it will most likely be through Jack Rabkinski. He won't be hard to find. I'll never understand what could have possessed your dear boy to take us to the studio, and more than that, it is totally incomprehensible that Rabkinski should have held still for it. It's crazy enough that Rabkinski should have been in on this thing, but for him to stick his head into the noose? Nothing will ever explain that. The man must have gone raving mad."

Alexandra dismissed the sculptor with a disdainful sniff.

"That one," she said. "I hope they do catch him. On just the bit of him I saw, I could tell that he was a brute and a horror, not to speak of your experience of the animal. But then, George, what was one to expect? Those things he calls sculpture? Of course, the man's a wild animal and an insane brute."

"Michelangelo he isn't," I said, "but his stuff has force, raw power."

"Nonsense. It's mad and it's brutal."

That was Alexandra's opinion, and she stuck to it.

As I expected, it was no time at all before the police caught up with Jack Rabkinski. When they did, both Alexandra and I were disappointed. For Alexandra it was that her belief that the Rabkinski constructions could be the work of only a brutish lunatic was shaken. For me it was because my conviction that by taking us to the studio our kidnappers had handed the police an open-and-shut case just fell flat on its face.

It took no more than a simple police inquiry at the gallery that handled him to locate the sculptor. He was in

Paris. He had gone there for the opening of an exhibit of his work at the Centre Pompidou. At the moment when Alexandra and I had been taken captive in the lobby of the Sandringham, Jack Rabkinski had been on a morning visit to the exhibit, inspecting with the curators of the Centre the installation of his sculptures in preparation for the opening scheduled for later in the day. You must remember the time-zone difference. What had been the wee hours in New York was, of course, mid-morning in Paris.

At the time when I was trussed up in the studio and being brutalized with my lunch, Jack Rabkinski had been in a Drouant private dining room being feted at a dinner in his honor. Reached in Paris with the news of the invasion of his studio, he had flown straight back to New York.

To some extent I had not been too far off the mark. In size and beef and brawn, he was by no means a bad match to the thug who had been my tormentor. He had the big, work-hardened hands, but his fingernails were decently short and well cared for. They had no jagged edges. There was also his voice and his speech. He was soft-voiced, astonishingly so for a man so burly and barrel-chested. His speech was not only cultivated, but to a conspicuous degree it was Boston accented. He held a Harvard A.B., and the Yard had taken over his tongue.

Alexandra had to concede that he was another charmer. She made the concession in her own manner.

"That," she said, "is what is so wonderful about men, the great dears. No matter how long an experience a woman might have of them—and for few women has the experience been as long as mine—there is always another unaccountable man to come along and astonish you. I

shall never understand how such a love of a man can produce those threatening steel horrors."

The police brought him together with Alexandra and
me, and we repeated for him our description of our kidnappers. Jane, of course, would have added nothing to
what we were telling him, but Jane, in any case, was not
available. She had lost no time about skipping town, and
she had left no forwarding address. Her reservation at
the Sandringham had been for only the one night, the
night of the Sandringham burglary and our kidnapping.

It could be assumed that the kidnapping had kept her
in town for a longer stay than she had intended since that
one night for which she had reserved had been followed
by the day and night in the Rabkinski studio, but it still
seemed fair enough to say that she had skipped town.

At the hotel she had registered from Pittsburgh. Since
the police were required to keep in touch with her against
the time when she might be needed as a witness, they
tried to locate her in Pittsburgh. They didn't find her. She
had been living there, that much they learned. But, on
leaving New York, she had evidently not returned there.
She had dropped out of sight and without even so much
as a day's delay. It figured. She was determined to evade
being called as a witness.

The session Alexandra and I had with Rabkinski was
fruitless. Such descriptions as we could furnish meant
nothing to him. He gave every evidence of trying, but he
said he was baffled. He could come up with no one who
would fit our descriptions even remotely.

The lock he'd had on his studio door could be described only as a feeble joke. A man would need no extraordinary burglary skills to fabricate a key that would
fit it.

"I never had the first thought of burglary," he explained. "The sculptures are big and heavy. It takes major equipment to move them. Nobody was going to come in and just lift them, and I've never had anything else in the studio that mattered."

He thought a moment and then he amended that.

"Acetylene torches," he said, "tanks of gas, tools. They took those, of course, but they put them back. I can tell about the gas. There are some empty tanks that I left far from empty."

The picture filled itself out. It had been no secret that Rabkinski was to have the Centre Pompidou show. Stories about it had been widely published. The thing had been all too easy. When Rabkinski had moved off to Paris, the gang had just moved in. Since the studio was unique for the block in which it was situated, everything else on the street being business premises occupied only during the day, the gang could come and go at the studio, and as long as they did it at night, there would be no one to see them. Rabkinski, when he'd taken off, had left the heavy draperies pulled across the windows. Obviously, they had been left that way till the very last and opened only after the man had switched off the lights as the last thing he did before he pulled out and left Jane and me.

Using the studio, they'd had no need for a place where they could keep the equipment they needed for the Sandringham job. More than that, they'd had no need for assembling the equipment. They could use Rabkinski's stuff. Police questions about the purchase of torches and other cutting tools would go nowhere. What I had taken to be stupidity to the point of madness had been just another clever facet of a well-organized caper. Even the kidnapping no longer seemed a silly improvisation. The gang had such a splendid hideaway. They had it, and it had been asking for a kidnapping.

They had taken us with only the one purpose. We were hostages useful for hampering any immediate pursuit. We had been held for the twenty-four hours only because time had been needed for moving the loot to some safe place, possibly also for a division of the loot. By the time that had been done and Rabkinski's tools had been returned to their proper places, it would have been well into the daylight hours when it would have been dangerous for them to show themselves out of the studio. Accordingly, they had remained holed up with Jane and me behind the studio's heavy draperies until we were again deep into the night and they had the greatest guarantee that the deserted street would remain deserted.

So far as Alexandra and I were concerned, it had become a closed episode. It could be expected to remain closed until such time as the police might come up with some arrests and we would be called upon to attempt identifications and to give testimony. I mean that so far as it might have been a question of any action, it was a closed episode; but Alexandra and I would need to have been something less than human for us to have not been plagued with continuing curiosity.

Alexandra was at the Sandringham. She had been living out of New York for some years. In preparation for returning to the city, she had bought an apartment. Since she was having the place redecorated, she had taken the room at the hotel. She was to live there till her new home would be ready for her.

Between us, therefore, we were admirably placed for picking up the tidbits with which we fed our curiosity. Even though burglary and kidnapping, since nobody had died, were out of Chief of Homicide Schmidt's area of professional concern, the inspector, as a highly placed member of the NYPD, had access to the day-to-day reports of police progress or lack thereof.

Alexandra, for her part, as a resident at the Sandringham, who as a result of the shared experience of their traumatic night had a special rapport with the hotel staff, was picking up every last morsel of hotel gossip. The loss claims put in by hotel patrons ran to astronomical sums. Everyone who had put anything at all into safe deposit was, of course, entering a claim, and it appeared to be the general assumption that at least some of the claims were padded. An envelope containing a thousand dollars in cash had been put in. If ten thousand was claimed, who was to say that the envelope had not contained that much?

Among Alexandra's gleanings, however, another aspect presented itself. Naturally enough, many of the hotel's guests were now taking a dim view of the security of the hotel's safe-deposit arrangements. Some people were taking boxes in banks one block over on Madison Avenue. Others were keeping their valuables always on their persons or seeking to conceal them in their hotel rooms.

One of the amenities of the Sandringham is afternoon tea served to hotel patrons. In fine weather the tea is served outdoors in the garden courtyard. Friendships develop over the tea cups. Inevitably the teatime conversation leaned heavily on an exchange of ideas about how valuables could be safeguarded. Alexandra reported hearing of a great variety of weird and wonderful hiding places people had thought up. An envelope taped to the back of a chest of drawers, a package wrapped in waterproof plastic and suspended in the water tank of the john, jewelry buried in a box of bath powder, jewelry hidden in a shoe, money concealed in a box of disposable diapers.

It never occurred to any of them that he was not the first to think up one of these dodges. I could tell Alexandra that they had all been used again and again. Hotel thieves knew them all.

"There's no place in the world where hotel rooms are safe from hotel thieves," I told her.

"I know that," she said. "It wasn't just the safe-deposit boxes that night. It was upstairs as well."

I thought she must be mistaken. I knew that for that date the police hadn't had any reports of thefts from any Sandringham rooms.

"Yes, but not reported, my dear."

"Then how do you know?"

"Yesterday at tea this little woman got talking, and since she's a ridiculous babbler, she came out with rather more than she meant to tell."

"She had a loss from her hotel room and she didn't report it? Why not?"

"Insurance."

"That's the world's best reason for reporting the loss."

"She's afraid they'll raise her premium or even refuse to renew her policy."

"That's silly. Why go to the expense of carrying insurance if you're going to take uncompensated losses?"

"But that's just it. She isn't."

"Isn't what?"

"Isn't not putting in a claim."

"But you just said . . ."

"I said she's not reporting the theft as from her room,"

Alexandra explained. "She's told her insurance man that it was in one of the boxes downstairs when it wasn't."

I laughed.

"The woman's an idiot," I said. "The hotel has its list of people who left things in safe deposit. If she isn't on the list, she can't possibly have a claim."

Alexandra explained it to me. The woman was on the list. She traveled with great quantities of jewelry, some to be worn by day and some to be worn at night, some to be worn with one color and some to be worn with another.

"You can't wear emeralds with a red gown unless you want to look like a gypsy," Alexandra said. "Surely you can see that, George, dear."

"It's a problem I've never had to face."

On checking into the hotel, Alexandra explained, this woman had taken one of the safe-deposit boxes and had deposited all her changes of jewelry in it with the exception of what she had to have on her lest she be insufficiently covered for checking into a hotel. Each time the color or the type of her toilette demanded a change of gems, she had gone to the box to deposit in it what she had been wearing and to take from it what she needed for the next ensemble.

"When she went out in the evening," Alexandra said, "I gather that she was as dazzling as a Christmas tree, and when she came back in she was too tired to cope. I can well understand that she would be very tired indeed after having labored all evening under all that mineral weight."

Evidently this Christmas tree of Alexandra's had been going to her room every night in full dazzlement and had done nothing about stowing away her nighttime adornments until sometime the next morning when she would get around to putting them back in safe keeping. On that night when the safe-deposit boxes had been hit she had, of course, lost everything she had in the box; but, in addition, she had lost the jewelry she'd worn that night and carelessly had left on the dressing table in her hotel room.

"So, you see, George, she's put in a claim for all of it, but she's telling the insurance people that it was all in the box since it really makes no difference. What was gone from her room would have been just as gone if it had been with her other things downstairs, and she wants the insurance people to think of her as someone who exercises the most prudent care. She's lying, of course, but she thinks it's a white lie. Not really. It's at least grayish. Don't you think?"

Whatever its color, it had the two of us wondering about the many other Sandringham patrons. Since for that night there were no reported thefts from Sandringham hotel rooms, it seemed not too unlikely that the one woman was not the only hotel patron telling small lies of one color or another. According to the hotel staff, of the gang we'd tangled with none at any time had gone above lobby level. It seemed possible, however, that the hotel people could have been mistaken about that, but on the other hand it seemed impossible that if our bunch had done rooms as well as that safe-keeping area downstairs, they would have done only the one room.

It was a couple of months before the police came up with anything, and then it was the arrest of the big goon, the one I'd mistaken for Rabkinski. Seeing him again and after I had come to know the sculptor, I realized that, but for both being big and heavy-muscled, two men could hardly have been more unlike.

The arrest had come about in the routine way, with the assistance of an informant. The big lug's name was Raymond, William Raymond, and the way Inspector Schmidt put it, he was the type of crook most frequently turned in by informants.

"These bimbos go around making themselves more enemies than friends," Schmitty said. "What can they expect?"

Raymond lost little time about doing the thing that may well have made him even more enemies. He talked. In the expectation that he could lighten his own sentence, he turned in his five companions in crime. Alexandra and I, of course, could do a positive identification on only the one of them, the kindly, gentle, allergic one whose face we had seen. His name was Dutton, Harper Dutton, and he had no previous record. It was difficult to believe that he had been involved in no prior crime. He had exhibited too great a degree of expertise in his handling of this one. It seemed more likely that he had never before been caught.

All of the others had previous burglary or robbery convictions recorded against them. The two men who had driven the cars appeared to be specialists in that department. Their records showed nothing but the driving of getaway cars. Their names were Sam Stevens and Ben Carlson. Carlson neither Alexandra nor I had ever seen. He had been the driver of the other car. Although we had seen Stevens, the driver of the car we'd been in, it had only been as an unmemorable bulk with a turned up collar and a turned down hat brim. We were no good for identifying him.

That left the other pair and on them we could testify only to size, shape, and voices. Both of them had spoken to us, and Alexandra and I were agreed on the sound of them. I never expected that would be enough to convince a jury beyond a reasonable doubt, and it wasn't. They both had previous burglary convictions, but there was nothing that could be brought against them but the information laid by William Raymond and our recognition of their voices. The jury found that insufficient. So Cal Gibbons and Arnie Peters—such were their names—won acquittals, and along with them Stevens and Carlson, the two drivers.

Only the two men went up—William Raymond for a minimum sentence, the reward for turning State's evidence; and Harper Dutton also for a minimum sentence. Alexandra and I were able to do that much for him. We both of us took the stand and, however reluctantly, identified him. Jane had chosen not to, and by dropping out of sight she had made her choice stick, but neither Alexandra nor I could feel we had a choice.

So far as either of us was permitted to on the witness stand, however, we testified to his more than considerate treatment of us and to our certain knowledge that, but for his intervention at his own great risk, there would have been three of us murdered in cold blood. It didn't weigh enough with the jury to win him an acquittal—it could hardly have done that; but, backed up with letters of appeal Alexandra and I addressed to the judge, it weighed enough with him to hold the sentence down to the minimum.

Notwithstanding the fact that we'd done all we possibly could in his behalf, the trial and the sentencing were a painful ordeal. They took much out of poor Alexandra, possibly even the more because of the way Dutton behaved throughout. He had nothing for us at any time but

smiles and pleasant, courteous greetings. It was as though
he were telling us, even in the moments when we were
pointing the finger at him, that it was all right, that he understood, that he felt that we were doing only what we
must.

Alexandra was shaken by it.

"He's reassuring us," she kept telling me. "He sits there
trying to buck us up. He's in desperate trouble, and he's
more concerned for us than he is for himself. I can't bear
it. He's everything a young man should be. How could he
have put himself in such a mess? Why? Why?"

Those, of course, were unanswerable questions. I was
wondering about it myself. Till the day she died Alexandra never forgot him. It seemed to me that he was
never far from her thoughts.

It was only a bare six months after the trial that she
went. There was nothing in it of cause and effect. She was
full of years, and they had to come to an end sometime. I
couldn't have wished her a better finish, and I never
wished her anything but the best. She went through her
last day completely herself, undiminished in mind and
body. That evening she was at the opera. It was *Don Gio-
vanni*, and in the moment when the *Commendatore* fas-
tens his granite grip on the Don and the orchestral sound
mounts mightily, Alexandra took her last breath. When
the singers came out for their curtain calls, the people in
the adjacent seats saw in the light reflected off the gold
curtain that Alexandra was slumped forward in her place.
She was dead.

Partly because she was Alexandra Gordon and mainly
because of the time and place of her dying, the newspapers gave her obituary considerable prominence. She
had many friends, and as was to have been expected, they

turned out for her funeral, but there was one face in the crowd I hadn't expected. It was Jane Harcourt. She spoke to me.

"I knew her how long?" she said. "All in all it was only minutes. Perhaps it was because what we shared were such emotional minutes, but I really don't think it was that. I think that wherever I might have met her, under whatever circumstances, I would have loved her at first sight. I wish it could have been more than just that one time."

"She took a great liking to you," I said.

"I had to go away," Jane said. "Not only go away. I had to drop out of sight. I thought I might stay, and if he was caught, I could say he wasn't the man. I think I would have done that if it had been me alone, but there was Alexandra and there was you. It couldn't have been any good, and I just couldn't stand it. So I never had any of the time with her I'd have liked to have had."

"These months since the trial was over?"

She sighed.

"I know. Time and again I thought of calling her, but then I thought how she must despise me and I couldn't."

"She never despised you. She often said she wished she could have done what you did. I can't say I didn't wish it myself."

She gave me her phone number and a couple of days later I called her. I took her to dinner. I had something I wanted to tell her because it seemed to me that in a way it spoke to the way Alexandra had felt about her. It was Alexandra's will. The bulk of her estate had gone to the Gordon Foundation. You've heard of it, but you probably wouldn't know that it was established by the grandfather of Alexandra's fourth husband.

There were, however, several bequests to people who had worked for her and to friends. She left me, for example, her books and a cash sum. What I wanted to tell Jane was something else—a bequest of ten thousand dollars to Harper Dutton to be held in trust for him till he came out of prison and to be turned over to him with accrued interest in one lump sum at that time.

When I told her, she caught her lip between her teeth and the tears came up in her eyes. She fought them down. She was not one who would permit herself to cry in public. I'm not at all certain that she was one to permit herself to cry anywhere or anytime. She took a moment or two to bring herself under control.

"Does he know?" she asked.

"He'll be having a letter from the attorneys if he hasn't already had it."

"He'll like that," she said.

It was obvious that she wasn't thinking that he would like the prospect of having the money. She was thinking that it would make him happy to know that Alexandra could have been that much taken with him and had felt no resentment.

"If it doesn't make him feel more guilty about what he did to her," I said.

She flared up.

"He didn't do anything to her. He didn't do anything to any of us. He was sweet and kind and he was protective of us. Those others, they were going to kill us. He could have let them do it, and he wouldn't be where he is now. He would have been safe—no witnesses. He sacrificed everything for us."

"Exactly what Alexandra and I told the judge."

She was quickly contrite.

"I know," she said. "And he knows. He liked her and he liked you. He still does. You're the kind of people he all his life wanted to know. That was what he wanted most in the world, to have friends like you. In a crazy way it was part of the reason why he kidnapped us. It was an unconscious reason, of course, but it was there. He liked us. He wanted to be with us awhile, and he could see nothing ahead but that he would never see any of us again."

"He tell you all that while we were in the studio?"

She flushed and dropped her eyes.

"Yes," she said in a voice that was only barely audible. Then she stopped and shook her head. Looking me in the eye, she spoke again. Now, though still low voiced, she was easily audible. "No," she said. "Not then. I've been seeing him since. I'm visiting him in jail as often as he's permitted a visitor."

"Oh?"

"Do you remember what Alexandra and I were talking about back then while they were holding us in the bar?" she asked.

"I remember you were both appallingly blithe. You couldn't have prattled away more merrily if you had been at a cocktail party."

"Would you have rather we'd gone into shrieking hysterics?"

"No, but hairdressers and health farms?"

She chuckled.

"You didn't finish alliterating," she said. "You stopped short of the important topic."

That had me thinking a bit and trying to remember. Alliteration helped me to my first glimmering of what she might have been about to tell me.

"Hairdressers and health farms," I repeated. "Yes, and husbands?"

"Interesting men and exciting men, men who aren't afraid to take dangerous chances. You run the risk of losing them, but they are worth the risk. They'll never bore you. Don't you remember her telling me that?"

"I remember," I said. "I hardly think she meant a man you'd have lost before you ever had him."

"Only temporarily. A minimum sentence and good behavior, it won't be forever or anything remotely like it before he's out on parole."

"And you've set your cap for him? You'll marry him when he comes out?"

"We had that one day and one night. It was hardly more than begun before I was madly in love with him. Then it was no time at all before I knew that he was in love with me. He said at first sight, and I realized it was first sight for me, too. Even though he looked ghastly and ridiculous with that awful stocking thing pulled over his face, I knew that if the thing came off and he would look totally hideous, it would make no difference. I was going to find him beautiful."

"None of my business but . . ." I said.

She laughed.

"What do you want to know?"

"Those hours in the studio—did you?"

"Of course. How not? We were in love, and as it looked then, those hours together were going to be all we might ever have of it. There I was—blindfolded and my arms strapped down to my sides and he doing everything for me. I don't have to tell you what everything was, but don't get to thinking that he raped me. If anything, it was the other way around. I raped him. There wasn't a chance that I wouldn't. I don't think there could be another man in the world who could have handled the whole thing with so much charm and tact."

"Charm and tact? If you can call it that, then you are in love."

"I know it sounds crazy, but nobody could imagine."

"He's a crook and a brilliant crook. Once he's out, do you think he can stay out of trouble?"

She shrugged.

"An interesting and exciting man," she said. "He's worth the hazards."

"Maybe, but you'll have time for thinking about it—until he gets out."

"No," she said. "We're already married."

"In the eyes of God or of the bathroom mirror?"

"Bell, book, and candle, not to speak of license and blood tests. We did it on my second visiting day. It's legal and official. I'm Mrs. Harper Dutton."

V

I was startled. I was seeing Inspector Schmidt the next day and I was full of it. I had to tell him. He took it very much in stride.

"Not as unusual as you think," he said. "The psychiatrists have a name for it. The shrinks call it the Something-or-other Syndrome, named after one of the cities in Germany where they first studied it. It was a case very much like this. A woman was held hostage in a robbery, and before he turned her loose, she had developed such a thing for the robber that she did exactly what this dame's done. She visited him in jail and they were married in jail. The only difference was that the woman over in Europe didn't dodge the trial. She took the stand and testified against the guy. It didn't stop her loving him or him her. These are extreme cases."

He went on to tell me about other less-extreme cases. A captive shut up with a captor for any length of time tends to develop a bond of sympathy with the kidnapper. If the conditions of captivity are too traumatic, of course, the bond is far less likely to develop, but obviously the conditions had not been traumatic for Jane. Schmitty went on to talk about the strong emotional aura that developed in any captive-captor relationship.

"There's a sexual angle to it," he said. "Captivity, that's a very sexy thing. If, as she says, he was gentle with her but at the same time was exercising complete power over her, they must have been having a very special kind of S/M thing—sado-masochism without pain. After all, in your own way—you and Mrs. Gordon—weren't you drawn to him?"

"For me he was the wrong sex."

"Of course, but still a strong liking," Schmitty insisted. "You did your part in getting him sent up, but you hated doing it."

"It's your job," I said, "but do you like that aspect of it, sending anybody up?"

Schmitty grinned.

"It's not the best part of the job," he said. "It never has been, but your feeling was different. It's a natural thing. It happens to cops all the time. It's one of the things you have to watch in police work."

"In what way?"

"You have a plainclothesman infiltrating a mob or maybe some pressure group that looks like it has a potential for going violent. It's good policy not to leave your guy out there too long. After three weeks or a month you want to watch it. There's always the danger that he'll be turned. People are too likable, Baggy. Even the worst of them—you get to know them well enough, and you catch yourself beginning to like them."

"I was talking to an anthropologist once," I said. "He told me just about the same thing. He'd worked with the aborigines of northern Australia. He said they were unattractive and had the most repulsive habits of any primi-

tive people. In his opinion you couldn't find people anywhere who would be less likable, but he assured me that
it made no difference. Living among them, he had come
to have a liking for them. He said it was hard to remain
impartial about any people you have studied. Anthro-
pologists always have to be alert against that kind of bias."

The inspector nodded.

"See," he said, "it's pretty much the same thing."

"Yes, but still to marry the guy in full knowledge of
what a bad risk he is."

"Why a bad risk?"

"You think he'll come out and go straight? Come on,
Schmitty."

"He just might. It's no lead-pipe cinch either way.
After all, he comes out and he's all set. He goes straight
from the slammer into the arms of a rich wife. The dame's
loaded, isn't she? They don't stay at the Sandringham if
they aren't, not even for one night. And there's more than
that. There's the easy way she comes and goes. She didn't
want to be around to testify against him, so she took off
and made herself unavailable. She hasn't been having a
job or a business, and she hasn't been wanting for bread.
It has to be she's loaded."

"No more capers? He'll just live off his wife's money?"

"It's been done. Maybe it's why he married her."

I shook my head.

"It could never be more than part of a reason. You've
seen her. She has looks. She's built. She wouldn't be hard
for any man to take. More than that, she's intelligent and
she's a good sport and good company."

"All that plus she's loaded and plus the ten grand and
interest from the old lady's will. Who comes out on parole
and has it that good? One of the reasons we have so many

repeaters, Baggy, is because life out on parole for most guys isn't enough better than life in the slammer. It won't keep them from taking the chances they hope will make it better. The figuring is that if they win, they have it made. If they lose, they're not losing much. Look at it this way. Who comes out on parole?"

"A guy who's behaved himself on the inside and who gives promise of being able to make it legally on the outside."

"The first half of that, yes," Inspector Schmidt told me. "The rest of it? Nobody believes that any more. The guy who behaved well on the inside is a guy who has demonstrated that he can adjust well to prison life. That's all. It says nothing about how well he can adjust to life outside. He's one who gets along great in prison. It's not too terrible for him to go back."

I winced. The inspector tossed me a questioning look.

"Yes," I said, "that's one of the things wrong with their marriage. He's behaving himself inside. She's got herself a guy who makes a good adjustment to prison."

"Maybe that says he'll make a good adjustment to marriage," Schmitty said. "And this marriage? Look at all he's got to come out to. A lot of the problem boys maybe would behave if they had half that much to look forward to."

Jane and I kept in touch. I liked her and I was curious about her marriage and what would come of it. Knowing the full score of how she felt and what she had done, I would have expected that she would have at least some small feeling against me. After all, I had fingered her man. I had testified against him; it was in some part my doing that he was where he was instead of eating at her table and sleeping in her bed.

I asked her about it.

"I did feel it at first," she said. "Not much, only a little, but there was that small bit of feeling. I told myself that you couldn't be expected not to identify him and not to testify at his trial, but I wasn't happy that you did. It was really Dutt who helped me rid myself of the feeling. He likes you and he admires you. It would give him a tremendous boost if sometime you would go up with me and visit him."

I did go with her, and I began to understand why she wanted to keep in touch with me. I knew him. I was someone with whom she could talk about him. I couldn't even begin to put on an act of being as delusional about him as she was, but that wasn't necessary. I liked the guy, and with every visit I made with her, I found myself liking him more. He was invariably bright and cheerful. He worked at cheering her up. He bent every effort toward making her laugh.

With me he was amazing. If either of us showed any evidence of embarrassment or constraint, it was I. He was always natural and warm, amused and amusing. His jail time wasn't hanging heavy on his hands. He filled it full. He was a painter and he was putting out a steady stream of canvases, drawings, water colors, pastels, gouaches. Her house was filling up with his works, and she trudged around town tirelessly with a portfolio under her arm. She was looking for a gallery that would give her genius a one-man show.

A genius he wasn't. He wasn't even greatly talented. All that could be said for his stuff was that he was hard-working, and it showed. I found his things hard to look at. I wondered whether they had been half as hard to paint.

With her, however, it was: Move over, Picasso. Step
down, Cezanne. Here comes the real stuff.

She raged against the blindness of the gallery and museum people who weren't rushing out to strip their walls
of all those lesser works to make room for the Harper
Duttons. Eventually she did get him a show, but it was in
a shabby basement gallery in a wrong neighborhood. It
wasn't the Village and it wasn't SoHo and it wasn't
Madison Avenue. It was the kind of gallery that never
sells anything. It exists on what artists or their families
will pay for the privilege of showing and on what they
can milk out of those same artists or artists' families over
and above what they should be paying for the printing
of a catalogue and for buying the wine to serve at the
opening.

Jane swore to me that she paid nothing for the show;
and, when I saw the publicity the gallery put out, I could
believe her. The whole of the play was that these things
had been painted in jail and that the artist was still behind bars. I'll grant you that there wasn't anything else
that could honestly have been said about the show, but
they so obviously played up the prison angle that I could
well imagine the gallery had considered it worth their
while to let her have the show for free. They would do it
for the publicity they could expect to get out of it. For the
first time they were going to have the name of their gallery in the papers.

They did better than that, however, because Jane was
determined that the thing should be done right. Instead
of the Jugoslav Reisling or California jug wine usually
served at openings in galleries of that sort, she went for
Heidsieck. Instead of settling for Xeroxed copies of a
typewritten list of the exhibits, she went for a beautifully

printed job. How much those gallery thieves skimmed off the top of what they charged her for those frills, I hate to think.

I expected the opening to be a disaster. The gallery had no following. Who was to come? I did what I could to soften the blow, working at getting everyone I knew to come to the opening. I told them they didn't have to buy even though the prices she put on the stuff would have been moderate if the stuff'd had any merit at all. All they had to do was look interested and find something kind to say. I could promise them that the champagne would be good.

So she had something of a crowd. None of the art critics came. The newspapers sent cub reporters who would be cutting their journalistic teeth on feature stories about the Slammer Cezanne. Nobody bought anything, so before the afternoon was over, I let my heart win over my eye and I went for a drawing. At least one little red star went up on a frame.

I was soon to come to regret it. Even though the press was just what I'd known it would be, day after day I had ecstatic phone calls from her. Another sale, and another sale, and then one day three sales all in one afternoon. Dutt was selling. He was going to be so happy, and he was going to be so proud of her because she had brought it off for him. Wasn't it wonderful? He was on his way.

I was thinking wonderful indeed. I dropped around on closing day, and sure enough, there were all those little red stars. A good half of the show was so marked. Not many artists do nearly as well on a first show. I picked up my drawing and I did have a moment of wondering where all those other buyers were. They'd bought, but none of them seemed to be hurrying around to haul their prizes home.

She could have had me fooled if I hadn't just happened on the truth of the thing. About a week after the show closed I spotted in the window of a Second Avenue thrift shop something that interested me. You know those places. People contribute old stuff to be sold for some charity or other. The thing I spotted was an antique set of brass knucks. I'm not kidding. They were rusty old iron ones and it seemed to me that, even old and rusty, they could still be effective and that they shouldn't be left there to fall into the hands of some kid who might put them to use. I also had the idea that they would be a gag gift I could give to the inspector.

I went in to buy them, and inside the place a painting caught my eye. There was no mistaking it. It was a Harper Dutton. I picked it up and discovered that it was the top of a stack of Harper Duttons, and not one of them I didn't know. They even had the little red stars still stuck to their frames. I counted them and the count was only one short. I'd heard from Jane again and again how many had been sold out of the show. They were all in that thrift shop, all but the one—and I knew where that one was. It was back in my apartment.

I went out of there with my brass-knuck purchase, and I was thinking that greater love hath no woman. I said nothing to her about it, though I had misgivings. I was wondering whether it was wise to be giving Dutt this big, phony build-up. Wouldn't there have to be a disastrous comedown?

I had the thought, but I wasn't worrying about it too much. I remembered how he had taken his trial and his conviction, and I thought about how he was taking his time in jail. There was a lot of cheerful bounce in the man. Nothing ever got him down. In the weeks that followed, however, I was often tempted to tell Jane that I knew and to show her that what she was doing wasn't too smart.

She was giving it the great build-up. Now it was the fault of the gallery people and the museum people and the art critics that her man was in jail. Here we had a man with such great gifts and nobody to give him the first bit of encouragement. Was it any wonder that he should have become embittered? Who, treated as he had been treated, would not turn against society? She wanted me to think how it would have been for me.

"Just think, George," she kept saying, "if, when you had written the first of your wonderful books, nobody'd even wanted to read it, much less publish it. . . . Think of that. Think of what it would have been like if it had happened with the first of your books and the second and on and on. Wouldn't you have turned as Dutt did? They don't want me constructive. All right. Let them have me destructive."

She couldn't have been more full of it. Now everything was going to be all right. Dutt had his foot in the door. This was only the beginning. He was going to come out and he would go from triumph to triumph. She was talking nonsense, of course, and she couldn't have not known it. Another show in that schlock gallery and another and another, and each one a triumph because she'd be in there surreptitiously buying the pictures and then getting them out of sight by dumping them on a thrift store? It was ridiculous. Dutt was a miserably bad painter, but he wasn't a blind idiot. For how long did she think she could keep him fooled?

I felt I should get down to cases with her about it and try to show her how she was heading her man down a road to nowhere, but I never could find a way of putting it to her, and I was telling myself that it could wait till he would come out and she started building for another exhibition. I was going to get to work on her then.

The time finally rolled around when he would be going before his first parole board. I told her that she ought to be doing something toward getting a job lined up for him. I was offering to check around to see what I could do in that direction.

"He doesn't need a job. He'll be working on his painting."

"That won't satisfy the parole board."

"Why won't it?"

"Because they operate under rules, and the rules aren't flexible. A man must have a guarantee of a job in properly legal and gainful employment before they'll parole him. It's an unavoidable prerequisite."

"He'll have gainful employment. You know how his things sold when I had the show for him."

"It's not a job."

"It's his job. It's his art. It's better than a job."

"Come on, Jane. It isn't and you know it isn't. I've put off telling you this, but you've got to be sensible. You see, I know just how things sold when you had the show for him."

"What do you mean?"

"I mean I saw them, the whole lot of them in the thrift shop where you dumped them."

Her eyes misted over with tears and valiantly she fought them back. Not a tear was permitted to fall.

"You won't tell him, George. Promise you'll never tell him."

"There'll be no need to tell him, but you've got to leave it that he just had that one success. It happens in art all the time. One season there can be a fad for a new artist. He does wonderfully, but then it's just a flash in the pan. It doesn't build, and it never happens again."

"But how can anything else happen if I don't ever again try to get his stuff seen?"

"He'll try. Leave it to him. My God, Jane, when he comes out, let him be his own man. Don't humiliate him. Don't emasculate him. Do you think that if he had been out and free to hang around the gallery you could have fooled him for a moment? He would have known what you were doing, and don't for a minute think I'm exaggerating when I say it would destroy him. Just believe me."

Whether she believed me or not, she switched. She did try to line up a job for him, but her effort took her only through a lot of futile motions. There was no place she could go. She knew no one but me. It seemed to me that when she had married Dutt, she'd cut herself off from everyone she had known before. She never said as much, but it didn't seem possible that she'd had no friends. That I was a friend came, I supposed, only from the fact that in a way we had shared him. She could be comfortable with me. I pictured her as probably being unhappily defensive with everyone else, and I had her tabbed for a girl who would fight off being forced into any kind of defensive posture.

I tried and it wasn't easy. It never is, but I lined up a couple of jobs he could have had. Jane would have none of them. In fact, she flew into a rage at the thought that I might go over her head and let him know about them.

They weren't good enough for him. He was her husband. He wasn't going to go out of her house every morning to go to any such mean, paltry job. How could I even consider them for Harper Dutton? I knew what he was. I knew his quality. There had to be a decent job for him somewhere.

There was, and it came to him through no effort of hers or of mine. He secured it for himself. When I heard about it, I had to concede that her Dutt was every bit the extraordinary fellow Jane insisted he was. It was an assistant's job in an art gallery, and not the dump where she had put on his show or anything remotely like it.

If there was one single top gallery in the city, this was the one. One of the major stars in that dealer's galaxy of high-priced artists was Jack Rabkinski. It was through Rabkinski that Dutton landed the job. He had written to the sculptor and asked him the favor.

From time to time I had been running into Rabkinski at one or another museum or gallery opening. He always hailed me as the man who had the most intimate knowledge of his art. He would roar with laughter as he proclaimed it a "painfully intimate knowledge."

The first time I encountered him after I'd heard about the job and how Dutton had secured the offer was after Dutt had been before the parole board, but while the board's decision was still pending. I commended him for his kindness and generosity.

He shrugged it off.

"The least I could do for a fellow genius," he said.

That staggered me.

"You've seen his painting?" I asked.

He shut his eyes.

"Please," he said. "Not his painting but his *chutzpa.*

I'm a genius at *chutzpa* myself; but for smooth and silken but nonetheless unmitigated gall, I'll never be in a league with him. Anything that great cannot go unrewarded. He'll do all right for the gallery, too. With his charm he can sell anything. Give him something that's really salable, like my crap, and watch him go places."

"All the same, it was damn nice of you."

"What about you?"

"Mixed feelings," I said. "He chose to take the risk and let me live. Also, working with Inspector Schmidt as I do, following the inspector around on his cases so I can write them up, I get to know a lot of criminals. The more you know them, the more hopeless the whole thing seems. Rehabilitation? It's hard to believe it isn't a laugh, and now here's a guy who looks as though he might make it."

"Harper Dutton?" Rabkinski was laughing so hard, he choked on the name. "Just give him time enough to learn the works, and he'll be ripping off the gallery."

"If you think that, why did you go to bat for him?" I asked.

He shrugged.

"Why not? The gallery rips me off all the time, every day and twice on Sundays. It'll be poetic justice. A man settles for that. There is no other kind."

"If you're right, it's going to be terrible for his wife."

"Terrible, schmerrible. What illusions can she have? The first time they met she was seeing him at his worst." He took time out from what he was saying. It was for a knowing grin and a chuckle. "Or maybe you're right," he said. "Maybe she does have illusions about him. You, with all your experience, you have them, and you also at the very start saw him at his worst. You have illusions about him and that's even without knowing how great he was in the bathroom."

So Harper Dutton came out on parole. She went up on the great day to bring him home. I asked her if she wanted me to go with her. She said no. She said that at the first they would want to be alone. That seemed reasonable enough. I stayed away from them. I did have my curiosity, but I was waiting for them to make a move.

I stopped in at the gallery a few days after his release. The stuff they had on exhibition was not my kind of thing, but I fed myself a lot of nonsense about keeping an open mind. The truth of it was that I was curious. I thought I might see him. I didn't. A few days later—it was just a week after his release—she called me. She told me that they didn't have him out on the gallery floor. That was to come later, but at the start they were keeping him behind the scenes, crating paintings for shipment, uncrating things that came in.

"He says it's all right," she said. "He says it's a good way to get to know the work of the artists they carry. He insists that it doesn't bother him that he is being wasted, but I think it's an outrage. They're just taking advantage of him because he's on this ridiculous parole and because he's so good-natured. He'll let anybody climb all over him."

"He's right," I told her, "and you're wrong. Don't work on him. The last thing you want to do is make him dissatisfied. It's a job and a good job. Even if they don't bring him out of the packing room for the whole of his parole time, it's better than back in jail. You have him with you. The two of you are together. Isn't that something?"

"It's everything. Our happiness—nobody could begin to imagine it."

"Okay. You have everything then. With everything you can afford to be patient."

"I'm not impatient for myself. I'm impatient for him. Do you know that the outrageous rules of this parole nonsense say that he has to stay right here in New York? He can't leave. He can't go anywhere."

"That's right. He has to stay in the jurisdiction. What's so terrible about that? You're here, and you said that's everything."

"Don't make fun of me, George."

"I'm not making fun. You and Dutt have it made. Don't push. You can spoil it, Jane."

"It's for him. Time is slipping away from us, George, and we're stuck here."

"Where do you want to go?"

"Europe. Paris, London, Rome, Zurich. American dealers are hopeless. Over there they'll appreciate him. We should be finding him a dealer."

"Jane, forget it. You gave him a show and you saw what happened. That was all right because he wasn't here to see it. What are you doing? Are you going to push and push until you confront him with a disaster?"

"In Europe it won't be a disaster. It's different over there. People in Europe know the difference between painting and pastrami."

"No, Jane." The time had come when I felt I had to tell her. "He's just not good enough. To have any kind of success in the arts, you have to be phenomenally good or phenomenally lucky. It's best if you can be both. There are thousands of painters who have far more to show than Dutt has, and nobody ever gives them a second look."

"If that's what you think, why did you buy one?"

"You're not the one to be asking that, kid. My reasons were much like yours. I just acted on a smaller scale."

"I don't believe you," she said. "I think you're being horrid, and I can't see why. He thinks the world of you."

"And I'm thinking of him, of his self-respect, of his happiness, of his safety. Who do you think art gallery people are? Most of them wanted to be painters or sculptors. They saw that they weren't going to make it, so they settled for gallery work."

"I won't have Dutt settling for second best. Whatever you say, I know he's phenomenally good. I'm going to move heaven and earth to make him phenomenally lucky."

"He's that already," I said. "He has you."

"Now you are laughing at me."

"Anything but. It's the way he feels, and that's what counts. Let him run out his parole. For that long at least don't mess up his contentment. What you want to do will just whip him into dissatisfaction, and I know what that will make of him."

"What? You think he'll go back to being a thief. Is that it? Say it. Don't just go on hinting around."

"I'm not predicting any exact way it will take him, but you'll be making him into a disaster looking for a place to happen. Take it slowly, Jane. Everything easy and hope he doesn't get bored and itchy. Don't push him into playing games with his parole. Thank God that he isn't getting any such ideas on his own. The last thing you ever want to do is put them into his head."

She didn't like that. She hung up on me, but then the next day she called again.

"I told Dutt I was mad at you," she said. "Of course, I

didn't tell him exactly why. I just said you were being stuffy about the parole business, insisting that he had to follow every one of the silly rules and to the letter. He said you were right, and he said he wouldn't let me be mad at you, so I'm not, but don't think it's because I don't still think you're a stinker. It's only because I'm an obedient wife."

"That'll be the day, baby," I said.

I was laughing, but she was laughing with me.

"You'll see," she said. "He wants to have a party. He wants to celebrate. He commanded me to invite you. He said he'd beat me if I didn't, and he'd ask you anyhow. I'm cooking a magnificent dinner, and you must come. There aren't all that many people we want to celebrate with. Without you it will be no party at all."

"You're speaking just for him, of course."

"I'm speaking for both of us. He tells me I must love you, George, and as I said, I'm the obedient wife. Surely you don't want him beating me?"

She did cook a great dinner, and it was a good evening. There was only one other guest, Jack Rabkinski. It was the first time I'd been in the house since Dutt had come out. It was a tiny old job down in the Village. It was like a doll's house. Even when she had been in it alone, it hadn't been too big for her. It was just the right size for two, but only for a two with an unremitting desire to be close. During the time she had been in it alone the decor had been strange. I could think of it only as schizophrenic. The house itself was one of those early nineteenth-century gems—all neatness, grace, and proportion. She had bought the place furnished and there wasn't a stick or a stitch that wasn't just right for the house.

All over the walls, however, she'd hung Dutt's em-

barrassingly feeble daubs. They would have looked out of
place anywhere. In that setting they had been monstrous.
Now that was all changed. The walls had been stripped.
There was not a painting anywhere. I was wondering
whether it could be that now that she had her man with
her in the flesh, she no longer had any need to keep his
works around her. I didn't wonder for long.

Dutt called attention to the stripped walls.

"Place looks a lot better than when you were here last,"
he said, "doesn't it?"

"Different," I said.

He turned to Rabkinski.

"Jane had every wall covered with my garbage," he explained. "Paintings. She insists that she thinks they're
good, but I'm going to educate her. Even in the eye of a
loving wife, they shouldn't look good."

She couldn't just leave it there.

"It's not only the eye of your loving wife," she said.
"There were all the people who bought out of your show,
including George, as a matter of fact."

She was challenging me, but Dutt spoke first.

"How about that?" he said. "It's not as though it had
been when I had you blindfolded. You did it with your
eyes open. What were you thinking of?"

"Jane told me that you were reading my books," I said.

He threw his head back and roared with laughter.
Grabbing me in a bear hug, he whacked my shoulder.

"Acts of friendship both ways," he chortled.

It was a happy evening. Dutt was in magnificent form.
He kept the warmth and the laughter going. Neither he
nor Jane made much effort to conceal their inability to
keep their hands off each other. It was as though during
his time in prison they had built so overwhelming a hun-

ger one for the other that they could never have enough of touching.

Those evenings became a regular thing. Dutt was happy with his job, and the gallery was happy with him. The time came when he did go out on the floor, and as Rabkinski had predicted, he was one of the world's natural salesmen. Of course, there aren't many paroled convicts who have ever had it so good. The job was all right, and he talked of it as possibly being the start of a career he felt would suit him well. Meanwhile he had a wealthy wife who kept him in the lap of luxury. Also, over and above his pay, which, once he began earning commissions, wasn't bad, he had Alexandra's ten thousand. I never knew whether Jane was paying all the bills or whether, as he began to earn, he was sharing them. I did know that every day he would come home with something for her—a perfect pear, a basket of wild strawberries, a gag apron to wear when they had Rabkinski and me to dinner. It said: "Who asked these tacky people?"

They were the happy couple. They were fortune's favorites. Everything was going their way and they had each other. From their strange and rocky start, they had built on physical attraction something that showed every sign of transcending the physical. I would have taken bets on their happy future, and I would have given odds.

I would have been wrong. I learned that the night I was wakened by a four A.M. call from Inspector Schmidt.

"There's been a 911 from your syndrome buddies," he said. "I'm going over. Do you think you want to meet me there?"

It took me a moment before I could register on "syndrome buddies."

"Jane and Dutt? The Duttons?"

"There's only one of them now, one and a body."

"Dead? Who?"

"Dutton."

"How?"

"I'll tell you after I've been there. I'll tell you if I know."

I was reaching for my clothes.

"I'll meet you there," I said. "Jane will need someone."

VI

She did, if only to keep her from doing something stupid in her rage. She was lashing out in all directions, and she was making no sense. Dutt had been murdered at her side in their bed. She had been afraid of it. She had never drawn even one serene breath. The fear had always been with her. She had tried—God knows she had tried—to make him safe, but that damned parole officer with his damned parole rules, he had stopped her at every turn. She wasn't going to forget it. He was going to be sorry for it. A lot of people were going to regret the day they were born.

She had wanted to take him away. She would have found a place for them where he would have been safe. I remembered, didn't I? Europe, and it wasn't permitted— he had to stay in New York. He had to stay here to report regularly to his parole officer. He had to stay here where his enemies could get at him. Someone was going to pay for this. If it was the last thing she ever did, she would see to it. Someone was going to pay.

It took no little doing to get her past all that and bring her down to anything that might resemble a coherent account of what had happened. The inspector worked at it, and I did what I could to help. I told her that she wasn't going to do anything. Whatever had to be done, Inspector Schmidt would do. Okay, she wanted someone to pay and someone would, but only if she would do her part, and it was her part to tell the inspector exactly what had happened and how it had happened. She was also to tell the inspector everything she knew. That was all that she had to do. The rest she was to leave to Inspector Schmidt. It was his job. He knew how to do it. With her help he would do it: someone would pay.

It wasn't easy. It came in scattered fragments, and Schmitty had to winnow those fragments out of the rush of hysterical nonsense in which they were embedded. From her rantings you could have thought that Harper Dutton's parole officer had come in through their bedroom window while they slept and had shot Harper Dutton through the heart.

"He was the killer," she kept saying. "I blame him. It's his fault. He can't evade the blame. I won't let him."

It was only when she had calmed down enough to put it that the parole officer had "as good as pulled the trigger," that the inspector began to get anything, and even then it wasn't much.

"He came in by the window," she said.

"You saw the man?" the inspector asked.

"Of course, I saw him. He was right there in the bedroom with us."

"You saw him come in?"

"No. I was asleep. The shot woke me."

"Then what makes you think he came in by the window?"

"It was open. He went out that way. I saw him go out.

I grabbed up the gun and fired at him; but, of course, I was too late. He was away."

Actually that was all she really had to tell. It was all she had seen. The noise of the shot had wakened her. She hadn't known it was a shot, not at the first. All she knew was that something had startled her awake. She had opened her eyes and saw the figure of a man. He was climbing out of the window.

"I couldn't understand Dutt not having wakened," she said. "I shook him to wake him. I really don't know why I did that. Did I think he'd go after the man? Did I even want him to go after the man? I don't know. I think it was just that I felt he would know what to do. He was the man in the house. It would have been wrong for me to do anything. I had to turn to him. I suppose it was habit. Dutt was so thoughtful, so solicitous. He did everything for me. I never thought how dependent he was making me with his strength and his concern. It was so marvelous, so warming."

Again and again there would be excursions like that. Again and again the inspector had to coax her back into the area of simple fact.

"You shook your husband and he didn't wake?"

"How could he wake?" she screamed. "He was dead."

"You knew he was dead? When did you first know? How?"

"I shook him, and I knew. He didn't stir."

"Then what did you do?"

"I switched on the light and I saw the blood. That's when I screamed."

She remembered screaming, but everything else she told the inspector was confusion. She wasn't even sure that she remembered making a 911 call. She had, but not

until after there had been a couple of other 911 calls that
reported a woman screaming.

"You were afraid this would happen?"

"I was afraid they would come after him. I couldn't believe that they wouldn't."

"They? Who are they?"

"The five of them, the five who were with him at the
Sandringham that night."

"Why?"

"They wanted to kill him that very next day. George
knows that as well as I do. You know it. They wanted to
kill the three of us, and they would have, too, if Dutt
hadn't been too smart for them."

"They thought you and Baggy were a threat to them
because you had seen Dutton's face. That was then."

Riding over her hysterical interruptions, the inspector
worked at explaining it to her. I don't know that he considered it of great importance that she understand. He
probably would have been more than content to leave
that effort to me; but I gathered that he was hoping that
if he could clear her mind of this unreasonable *idée fixe*,
he might solicit from her something that could be useful
in the investigation.

He argued that any feeling the gang might have had of
being threatened by the three of us—Jane, Dutt, and myself—would necessarily have become a thing of the past.
The worst had happened. They had all of them been
apprehended and four of them had suffered no penalty.

"They were afraid," Schmitty explained, "that you people could finger Dutton, and that when he was arrested,
he would lead the police to the rest of them. It didn't happen that way. An informant gave us William Raymond,
and it was Raymond who turned in the rest of them. The

fact that you'd seen his face, that he'd let you live, that he'd tricked them out of their chance to kill you and him made absolutely no difference. At least it made no difference to the five others. They didn't suffer by it. Dutton was the only one who did."

She wouldn't be convinced.

"It's all very well for you to say that an informant gave you Raymond, and that he turned in the rest," she said.

"I'm not just saying it. That's the way it was."

"But who was the informant?"

That was a question the inspector couldn't answer. I doubt that he would have answered it if he could. It is police policy, wherever possible, to preserve the anonymity of informants. Exposure inevitably destroys an informant for any possible future usefulness, and it may also expose him to retribution. Since robbery is not in the inspector's department, he'd had no direct involvement in the investigation of the Sandringham job and of our kidnapping. The information on Raymond had come to a detective in the Burglary Squad, and the identity of the informant was his secret and his alone. Whether he had shared it with other officers on his squad or with the DA's office, the inspector didn't know. He had not shared it with the inspector.

"And much less with anyone outside the Police Department," Jane said.

"That's so," Schmitty agreed.

"So what's to prevent their thinking that you got to Dutt through Alexandra and George and that it was Dutt who informed on the rest of them?"

"What's there to make them think that?" Schmitty asked.

"They had it fixed in their minds that it was the only

way they could be caught. So then they were caught, and nothing would ever convince them that it hadn't happened that way."

"Four of them have been none the worse for it," Schmitty reminded her. "So that leaves Raymond. He may be out of jail. We'll be checking on that, of course, but he knows that Dutton didn't turn him in. He knows it was the other way around. He turned Dutton in."

She was still refusing to be convinced.

"If it had been Dutt who turned him in," she argued, "you wouldn't have told him. When he gave you Dutt, you acted as though he were giving you something. That would have been to protect Dutt. Raymond didn't know who turned him in, so he fastened on Dutt because he'd been living with the idea that if it ever came, it would come that way."

"Makes no sense," the inspector told her. "The judge gave him a minimum sentence because he had informed on the other five. Why would he get that if we'd already had the information from Dutton?"

"What makes you think that animal would make sense? George was the one who had experience of him. Ask George." She turned to me. "Would you expect him to make sense?" she asked.

The inspector wasn't waiting for me to come up with any answer. He had another argument to offer.

"There's another thing," he said. "If Raymond is out of jail, then he's served his sentence and he's in the clear. What gain would there be for him in killing Dutton?"

"To get even. The man's an animal, and anyhow we don't know that he's served his sentence. He may have escaped."

"Escaped to murder Dutton? What good would that do him?"

"A vengeful animal."

"You can't think of any better reason, Mrs. Dutton?"

"What could I know of an animal's reasons?"

"Your husband knew these men. What did he tell you about them?"

"He said they were stupid, violent animals."

"Nothing else?"

"Nothing else."

"And you've been living in fear of them in a ground-floor bedroom with no bars on the window."

"It worried me, but I couldn't do anything about it."

"You couldn't?"

"Have you no imagination, Inspector? Dutt had been living behind bars. Would he want them on the outside? Did he need such reminders?"

"All the stuff that was taken from the Sandringham that night—not even one piece of it has been recovered. Did your husband know what became of it?"

"He told everything he knew. The others made off with it and disappeared. They were cutting him out of it. He never saw any of them again until he was arrested."

"It was Raymond's story that your husband got the other five out of the way and made off with the whole of the loot, keeping it all for himself. Now if that was the way it was, or even if Raymond had any reason to believe it was that way, it could be he came here for his share."

"You know what Dutt swore to."

"It wouldn't be the first time a man swore to something and then told his wife something else."

"The police had that animal's story and they had Dutt's story. I don't know which they chose to believe. All I know is that I believe my husband. He never lied to me."

"And he told you—?"

"What he told the police."

"He managed to get the ammo out of all their guns and then, when his was the only loaded gun around, he got them away from the studio at gunpoint? Having such beautiful control of the situation, he just let them get away with the total proceeds of the big Sandringham job? Come on, Mrs. Dutton. Only an idiot . . ."

She sobbed.

"No," she said, "not only an idiot. Only my Dutt."

She came up with an extended argument, and I, who had been there, couldn't say that she was remembering anything wrong or putting a warped interpretation on anything.

Harper Dutton had made his mistake. He had committed his crimes. He had never denied them, and she was not about to deny them either. She had her ideas of how he had been driven to it, and she fed those to the inspector. That part of it, of course, was nonsense—all that stuff about his great genius and how he had been embittered and temporarily had lost his head because he had gone unappreciated. She tossed it all in, but she didn't labor it. She even conceded that it made no difference. However great his provocation, however shabbily he had been treated by society, he had done the wrong thing. He had turned to crime. She would never put another name to what he'd done. The Sandringham job was a crime. Carrying the three of us off as his prisoners was another crime.

"Of those things he was guilty, and for those things he paid. But the moment he had that allergy attack, everything changed. He became a different man."

"That's handing a lot to histamine," Schmitty said. "In a flash it transforms a man's character completely."

She glared at the inspector. She was shaking with anger. For a moment I thought she was going to hit him. She worked at getting control of herself.

"It's no good talking to you," she said.

"You want his killer caught," Schmitty reminded her.

"And you're the man to do it? No. You're too stupid, too much the prisoner of your stupid policeman prejudices."

Schmitty grinned at her.

"You're going to have to make do with me till a smarter cop comes along," he said.

"I don't think you'll understand," she said. "I don't think you're capable of understanding a man's finer feelings."

"Try me."

"He was a criminal, but he wasn't an animal. He was a man, gentle and kind and decent. He was incapable of hurting anyone, certainly incapable of killing or even of standing by and permitting a killing. He couldn't do that if his life depended on it, much less since it was only his liberty at stake."

She amended what she had said about his transformation in terms of becoming a different man. There was no change of character. He'd remained the man he had always been, a man of fundamentally decent priorities. What had changed was his situation. Up to the point when the allergy attack had forced him to tear off his stocking mask, the priorities had been to pull off the Sandringham job successfully and then, by taking us along as hostages, improve the chances of a safe getaway for his companions and himself.

"He knew the animals he'd been working with," she said. "He knew that if they saw the slightest advantage in it, they would kill us and never turn a hair, and he knew that they were seeing an enormous advantage in it once we had seen his face, and they, as a result, were feeling themselves endangered."

It was her argument that in the one moment his priorities shifted. The first priority became the prevention of these crimes he couldn't be part of and couldn't countenance, three murders—Alexandra's, Jane's, and mine. In the face of that great imperative everything else paled.

"That was immediate," she said. "When he let Mrs. Gordon go, he was doing it over the protest of the others. It was even worse than that. One of his goons was about to shoot him right then. It was only thanks to George that he didn't manage it."

None of this was new to the inspector, but he let her go on with it. My action, when I came to Dutton's aid in the car, she argued, strengthened this new priority of his. Now it was more than his nature and his principles. Now he'd been feeling that he owed me.

"Meanwhile," she added, "he was falling in love with me. You know about that, too, and whatever you think about it, I don't care. I'm not ashamed of it."

Eventually she came to the point she was trying to make. In love with her and feeling grateful to me, he came to the place where nothing mattered but his responsibility to the two of us. He had put our lives in jeopardy, and at any and all cost he had to save us.

"His share of what they had stolen became unimportant," she said. "He knew that they would make off with it and his whole effort would have been for nothing. He was never going to see them or any of it again, but that

was all right. He was calling it the price he was paying
for our lives. He knew that if he drove them away from
the studio, they would be right back to gun us down; but
if he drove them away with all that money and jewelry on
them, they would be so intent on getting away with the
loot and taking it to a safe place that they wouldn't even
think of coming back to kill us."

Schmitty shook his head.

"So why now?" he said. "If it had been the other way
around, if he had done them out of the haul . . ."

She had that all figured out. Dutt had sworn that the
others had the loot, and they had sworn that Dutt had it.
She put it up to me. I knew them. Given this choice between believing Dutt and believing the others, could
there be any question? Had any of the others shown even
the slightest symptom of decency? Wasn't it obvious that
they would have to be the liars?

"I can see the whole thing perfectly," she said. "They
hated him. They all hated him always. It was just because
of what he was, just being so much more intelligent than
they were, so much better in every way. It made them
feel inferior, and you know what they're like, George.
They have no answer to their inferiority feelings but vio-
lence. Nothing could be more obvious than that."

After this her argument turned a bit complicated. The
insurance companies were still looking to recover. On a
thing like that Sandringham job insurance companies
never give up. They'd all been having insurance company
detectives on their backs. She knew about that. She knew
how Dutt had been harassed by those investigators.
Since the five hated Dutt, they were saying that he was
the one who'd gotten away with what they wanted. They
were just the kind of animals who would think that if

they murdered him, it would convince the insurance detectives that it was because he had cheated them out of
their shares that he had been knocked off.

If Inspector Schmidt was listening to any of that, it was
only with half an ear. The inspector had taken Jane out of
the bedroom and had settled her in the living room. One
of his men had come to the door and Schmitty had joined
him there where they whispered together while Jane kept
pouring her argument at me. He came back to us, carrying two things—a revolver and a nylon stocking that was
grossly pulled out of shape and that had two eyeholes cut
in it. Jane's gaze fell on the stocking. With a gasp, she
stopped short.

Of course, she recognized it. Neither she nor I could
have been mistaken about it. It was impossible that either
of us should ever have forgotten that moment when
Harper Dutton, coughing and sneezing and strangling,
had ripped off his stocking mask and let us see his face.

"Where did you get that?"

Her voice came in a strangled whisper. She had to fight
to bring it back under control.

"You've seen it before?" the inspector asked.

"Of course, I've seen it before. They were all wearing
them that night."

"This one?"

"Ones just like it. Maybe he kept his. Maybe he made
himself a fresh one. What difference can it possibly
make?"

"Who?"

"Him. The murderer. Who else? He must have been
wearing it. I saw him throw something behind him in that
moment when I saw him going out of the window. He

must have pulled it off and left it instead of going out into
the street with it on. Here in the Village it's not like Fifth
Avenue outside the Sandringham. Down here people are
much more in the streets at night, even late at night. He
was taking no chances on being seen in the street wearing
that thing."

"It was found under the bed."

"I must have kicked it there. I remember running to
the window to stick my head out and scream for help and
then running back to Dutt, back and forth, I don't know
how many times. One time or another I must have kicked
it under the bed without even knowing it."

"Easy enough to do," Schmitty said. He indicated the
gun. "Ever see this before?" he asked.

She winced.

"I thought it would help," she said.

It was again the strangled voice and again the struggle
to bring it back up to audibility.

"Yours, Mrs. Dutton?"

"Technically mine. Dutt couldn't have one. It was
those idiotic parole rules again. I thought I could get
around that one, but I needn't have bothered. It did no
good. The rat never gave him a chance to use it."

"It not only did no good, Mrs. Dutton, it may well
have done harm."

A chill touched me and with it a rush of pity. She was
slower to pick it up.

"Don't lecture me, Inspector," she said. "What harm?
He had no chance to fire it."

"But it was fired."

She moaned. It was a moan of impatience and exasper-
ation.

"I told you I grabbed it up and fired at the man, but I was too late. He had gotten away."

"You fired at the man. How many shots?"

"One. Just one shot. He was gone, and it came to me that Dutt wasn't stirring. I'd climbed all over him to reach over to grab the gun. That hadn't wakened him and now the shot hadn't wakened him. It had to be there was something wrong with him, something terribly wrong. I dropped the gun and switched on the light. That's when I saw the blood and started screaming."

"It was on the bedside table, ready to your husband's hand in case of need. Do you know if it was fully loaded?"

"It was full."

"You know that?"

"I wouldn't be saying it if I didn't know."

"How do you know?"

"I loaded it."

She was off again on the parole officer who had as good as pulled the trigger. Dutt couldn't own a gun: that was one of the crazy parole rules.

"He never touched it. Of course, the idea was that he would have if it became necessary." She choked up on that. Pulling herself together, she amended it. "He would have if he could."

"Then if you loaded it full, Mrs. Dutton, and you fired only one shot, we have the bullet you fired. The boys are digging it out of the window frame. You missed the window. But there's a second bullet gone out of it. We don't have that one yet."

Her eyes widened. She caught her lip between her teeth. She was biting down so hard that I was expecting to see blood spurt out.

"Unendurable," she said. "You mean with his own gun —with my gun?"

"We won't know until the Medical Examiner gives us the bullet and ballistics has checked it against the revolver," the inspector said, "but for now it looks like it was fired twice. So unless you fired more than one shot and one went out of the window . . ."

She shook her head.

"No, only one shot. The ultimate cruelty to do it with the gun I bought for him, the gun I gave him to keep him safe."

It was the world's oldest story. The householder who keeps a loaded gun at his bedside and doesn't realize that an intruder will always have the jump on him because the sneak attack always has the jump on the defense. Keep a loaded gun like that, and the odds are always good that if anyone gets shot, it is going to be you.

Ballistics, of course, came through with the verification. The two bullets matched up. The slug the ME took out of Dutton's body and the one dug out of the window frame had both been fired from the revolver that had lain all too handy on the bedside table.

A check of the records, furthermore, revealed that William Raymond, having not been the model prisoner Harper Dutton had been, had been granted no parole. He had, however, served the whole of that minimum sentence imposed on him, and on the night of the shooting he had been six days out of prison.

It was the police lab, however, that came up with the staggering report. They had done an exhaustive work-up on the stocking mask that had been kicked under the bed. They had found hairs caught in the mesh and had been able also to draw out of it some dried sweat and dried saliva. On the basis of every test they could give it, they were asserting unequivocally that it had been worn over the head of Harper Dutton. It was his hair, his sweat, and his saliva.

VII

The word was out on Raymond. He was wanted for questioning. The boys were also doing a rundown on the other four. Meanwhile, Jane had been turning the house inside out. There was the one question the inspector had asked her for which she'd had no answer. She hadn't known whether there was anything missing, so now she was dead set on giving the inspector an answer. She was doing an all-out inventory.

The ways in which a woman might react to the shock and the grief of such sudden widowhood are manifold. They are as various as are women themselves. Some go into shock and need to be roused before they can begin to deal with their grief. Some take the edge off sorrow with a great vengeful anger. Some go limp and need to have everything done for them. Some go into a frenzy of activity—they busy themselves with every possible chore, and they bring to the doing of each chore the highest degree of intensity.

That was the way Jane was the morning following Dutt's death. She was whizzing about the house, wearing herself out, burying herself in activity. Maybe activity

can block away thought and pain. If it wasn't doing as
much for her, it wasn't for want of trying.

You know about my long-standing arrangement with
Inspector Schmidt. Any time he has a case that looks as
though it might develop into something worth my record-
ing, he keeps me at his side, giving me the opportunity to
see and hear at firsthand. On this one, of course, there
was a double reason. This one, after all, had been my case
long before murder came into it and made it the inspector's as well.

I was with him when the word came through that
Raymond had been located, and I went with him when
he went uptown to question him. Apart from the fact that
this questioning was inevitably going to be part of the
story, I had a special interest in William Raymond. If I
have ever known a man I had reason to hate, this was the
one.

The address Schmitty had for him was a tenement in
the East Nineties. It was a decent tenement, one of those
that still showed the scrubbed and starched-curtain ap-
pearance of workers' housing; it had not yet slid into the
slovenly decay that comes with the hopelessness and sur-
render of unemployment and Welfare.

One could, notwithstanding, hardly fail to mark the extreme contrast between the circumstances Raymond had
come into on his release from prison and the luxury that
had surrounded Harper Dutton. I was telling myself that
it signified nothing. It was no more than the difference
between what a convict could do for himself immediately
after he'd finished serving his term and what a convict,
released into the hands of a rich wife, could have done for
him by that devoted mate.

Just seeing the place from the street, before we ever

went inside, the contrast started me thinking. Someone had gotten away with the Sandringham loot. It had been Dutton's story that while he had been protecting Jane and me and himself from the murderous intentions of the other five, they had made off with it.

It was Raymond's story—the others had never admitted to anything—that, finding themselves unarmed and facing Dutton's gun, they'd had no choice but to do as he'd demanded and that he had driven them off empty-handed, keeping the whole of the take for himself. It occurred to me that it may not have been this simple choice of alternatives. If even one of the five had been squeezed out and didn't know precisely by whom, he might all too easily, on seeing the way Harper Dutton had been living, have jumped to the conclusion that it was the Sandringham take that was keeping Dutton in caviar and comfort.

Even if they knew that Jane had married him, there had been nothing to indicate that night at the Sandringham and through the hours after it that she was more than moderately affluent. She had been well dressed and well groomed, but she'd been wearing no jewelry at all. I could well imagine that there wasn't one in the five capable of conceiving of the possibility that a woman might be loaded and choose to spend her money in other ways. There was also his $10,000 bequest from Alexandra, of course, but none of them would have known about that. It seemed a cinch that if any of them was out in the cold and left to wonder which of them had the Sandringham take, he would inevitably assume it was Harper Dutton.

In the tenement vestibule the inspector found a bell marked with Raymond's name. He rang it. While we waited for an answer, I told the inspector what I had been thinking.

"It would be quite understandable," I said. "What I can't understand about it is the uselessness of the killing. You'd think they'd be letting him live and putting the screws to him to force a division."

The inspector tried the bell again.

He shrugged. "It seems obvious that Dutton was the brains of the operation," he said. "He seems to have been all the brain they had. You spotted him from the first as the man in charge, and all through the caper he was in command. That day he was the one who had the ideas. The rest of them couldn't come up with anything to cover themselves but the simple reaction of killing. Even then— five against one—he outsmarted them."

The inspector made a third try at the bell. This time he put his finger on it and left it there, leaning.

"You think it might be," I asked, "that they would be feeling so defeated by him that they would despair of ever coming up with anything but the short end of the stick if they tangled with him?"

"Why not? They get to thinking there's nothing they can do with him. He'll always get the best of them. That's a rotten feeling. A feeling like that can poison a man. It leads to thoughts like 'There's still one thing I can do. I can murder the bastard.'"

"And kiss off forever all hope of getting what they had coming to them?"

"I've known it to happen," the inspector said. "Take one of these violent types and frustrate him enough, anything can happen, and more likely than not it'll be something that's not in his interest."

His non-stop ringing finally brought results. We heard

the buzzing of the lock release on the vestibule's inner door. Schmitty pushed the door open. In the inner hall I could hear the voice I knew all too well. He was roaring down the stairwell, telling us we better have a good reason for all that bell ringing because it wasn't going to take much before he'd tear us apart with his two hands and feed us piece by piece to his neighbor's dogs. I could also hear the dogs. Their barking would have drowned out the words of any lesser man. As it was, his were only barely coming through. The dogs sounded hungry.

"That would be one way to tackle this case," I said, as we started up the stairs. "Find the one who has the loot, and you have him eliminated from your list of five suspected killers."

"Could be easier to do it direct," Schmitty said. "Just find the killer. There's another angle to this. You talk about the killer kissing off forever any chance he might have of getting his share."

"If that's why Dutton was killed, certainly," I said.

"Nothing certain about it, Baggy. If any of them think Dutton kept all of it for himself, then with Dutton dead, they're thinking it goes to his widow. How about somebody thinking she'll be easier to handle? What's to say that the pressure won't be coming down on her now?"

"Oh, come on," I said. "If it comes to her, that'll be the first she's ever known of it and, of course, she'll turn it in. I don't believe that Dutton had it, but if, for sake of argument, he did, then nobody will ever know where he stashed it. The secret will have died with him."

Schmitty laughed.

"It can look that way to you," he said. "Never to any of those crooks."

"Then she's in danger?"

"She might be, but they won't be trying to murder her. Nobody can be that stupid."

It was the top floor, five flights of stairs. By the time we were about to start up the last of the five the shouting from above was taking another turn. The dogs had fallen silent. It hadn't been from exhaustion. It had been on command. The order had come in a woman's voice. We'd heard it. It was the voice of a drill sergeant. Now that there are women in the armed services all over the world, it shouldn't be too hard to believe a contralto drill sergeant.

Having dealt with the dogs, she had, by the time we were mounting that last of the five flights, turned to tongue-lashing Raymond. She didn't like his language, she didn't like his bellowing, and least of all she liked his lack of modesty. She was telling him it was a decent house, decent people lived there—honest, hard-working people, not people with filthy habits.

There were smells drifting down the stairs that were verifications of what she was saying. There was the warm, yeasty smell of home-made bread in the baking. There was a mouth-watering stew smell. There was an apple-cinnamon-butter fragrance that could speak for nothing but mom's apple pie in the oven.

It had to be that she had opened her kitchen door to deal with her neighbor. It seemed wildly unlikely that William Raymond could have been performing those prodigies of cooking and baking.

We came up the last flight and they were there. She was quite as expected: flour-smeared hands, apron, hips, and bosom. He, but for a pair of jockey briefs that seemed even briefer than their name promised, was naked. His neighbor was berating him for indecent exposure. If it narrowly missed being indecent, it was obvious that to her eye the margin of miss was too narrow.

He was answering her, and what he was saying was more salacious than original. The guy had a limited mind and a restricted vocabulary. I'd had a hunch that on our trips to the bathroom I'd been hearing all the words he knew. Hearing him now, using them in this different context, my hunch was reinforced.

The very first moment I was far enough up the stairs for him to see more of me than just the top of my head, he knew me. Recognition was instantaneous.

"You," he chortled. "Need help with your zipper?"

The inspector took over.

"William Raymond?"

"Who's asking?"

Schmitty told him who. He seemed to be needing a little time for registering on it. His neighbor was quicker. She also jumped to an unwarranted conclusion. Assuming that the police in the person of Inspector Schmidt had come to put the arm on her neighbor on a charge of indecent exposure, she applauded our arrival. She volunteered to give us a statement. She assured us of her readiness to go to court whenever called and testify against this pig who had come to live among decent, respectable people.

"Always out in the hall like that," she said. "Always like that with nothing on. It's a scandal."

Raymond cut in on her to speak for himself.

"What do you want from me?" he said. "I'm clean."

At that moment in that place it wasn't the most fortunate choice of words.

"Clean?" his neighbor said. "He's a pig. Look at him—his hands, his feet. Does he look like he ever washed? You can smell it on him, like he's never had a bath. And he says he's clean."

Raymond came up with a threatening hand. The outraged housewife never retreated an inch. She just stood there regarding the huge hunk of meat and bone that served the man for a fist as though it were something offered to her in a butcher shop that was about to lose her patronage.

Schmitty intervened.

"If you will excuse us, madam," he said.

"Gladly, Mr. Policeman, gladly. Take him away. Keep him a good long time. Nobody here'll miss him."

The inspector turned to Raymond.

"Let's take this inside," he said.

"Take what inside? I ain't done nothing."

"Okay. So we'll talk about the nothing you ain't done."

I called it a decent tenement. Decency stopped at the door to Raymond's flat. Everything that his neighbor had been saying about the thug's person could also be said about his noisome nest. On the date we had for his release from prison it was obvious that he couldn't have been in that flat as much as a week. It didn't seem possible that any one man could have accumulated so much nauseous litter in so short a time. The place was strewn with empty bottles, dirty dishes, and filthy clothes. The materials that had gone into those clothes were of the sleaziest, but dirt had given them body. The place reeked of food gone bad and sweat gone sour.

Schmitty shut the door behind us. Raymond's outraged neighbor was still out in the hall. We didn't need an audience. The inspector began by reading Raymond his rights. Raymond paid scant attention. He'd heard them too many times before.

"Got a job?" Schmitty began.

"Yeah."

Schmitty looked at his watch. It was midmorning.

"Not working today?"

"I worked. I been sleeping. You woke me up."

"When did you work?"

"Night. Like always. Night."

I thought of the job at the Sandringham. That could have been called night work.

"What kind of a job? Where are you working?"

"Hunts Point Market, unloading the trucks."

Hunts Point is the wholesale vegetable market. It's up in the Bronx.

"Hours?"

"I show there eleven o'clock at night. I get paid off around seven."

It's not every night that one individual trucker or wholesaler up in the market will need any extra help, but they all work with minimum staff and on a night when one or another of them needs extras he picks them up from the bums, the vagrants, the unemployed, and the underemployed who hang about the market for a night's work. It's not regular employment. They're not on any-one's payroll for a weekly wage, but almost any night a man with a strong back can pick up a night's work some-where in the market.

"Every night?"

"A night I don't feel like it, I'll take me a night off."

"When did you last take a night off?"

"I ain't taken any nights off. Not none. Not yet."

"The night before last."

"I already told you. I ain't taken any nights off."

"The night before last, you were up there working?"

"Yeah."

"Time? From what time to what time?"

"Like always."

"Never mind always. That night?"

"I showed there eleven o'clock like. I got paid off it was a little after seven."

"And worked straight through?"

"Nobody works straight through. You take yourself a breather—a cigarette, a cup of coffee, a hamburger, a hunk of pizza. Nobody works straight through."

"All right. You take breaks now and then. Where do you go for these breaks?"

"Where all the guys go."

"Where's that?"

"By the coffee stand."

"So the whole time, eleven to after seven, you were up there. You didn't leave the market for any part of the time?"

"I was working."

"Did you leave the market for any part of the time?"

"I told you. No."

"You know what happened the night before last?"

"I unloaded lettuce."

"What happened down in the Village?"

"What happens every night down in the Village? It's always the same. It's fags grabbing for zippers. You want to know about that stuff, ask him."

He was, of course, indicating me. Inspector Schmidt wasn't interested.

"Your old buddy, Harper Dutton," he said.

"That son, he ain't never been no buddy of mine."

"Okay. Not your buddy. What have you got against him?"

"I got plenty."

"Like what?"

"Like that night we done the hotel. We was going to split even, six ways. There was never no split. He done all of us out of our shares. We never seen a dime, and that ain't all. He ratted on me. The cops, they said not him, but I know better."

I knew he was dumb, but I couldn't believe this dumb. He was volunteering all this stuff and there was nothing it could possibly have been saying to Inspector Schmidt except that William Raymond had motive aplenty for the murder of Harper Dutton. There was only the one way I could read it. He knew himself to be so solidly alibied for the night of the murder that he thought he had no need to watch his tongue.

"Night before last," Schmitty told him, "somebody iced Harper Dutton. Just one good shot, and it got him in his sleep."

Raymond blinked and gulped. His face was so much marked with broken veins that it couldn't show much in the way of a change of color, but there was a change. He paled. At the same time, however, there was a curious change in his demeanor. He tensed and a gleam came into his eye. It wasn't a wary tensing.

It was more as though his every muscle had gone on the alert for action. The gleam seemed baffling. On what he had been saying about Dutt, I could have expected some measure of vengeful joy. It wasn't that. It seemed more like hope, like eagerness. The vengeful joy was there as well, but it was only in his words. His mind was on something else.

"Why not?" he said. "Cheating shows."

"You didn't know?"

"How would I know? He leave me a million bucks in his will?"

"Newspapers, and it was on TV."

"You see a TV here?"

There was no TV. There were no newspapers either.

"In a bar?"

"I go to a bar, I drink. I don't look at no TV. I don't go for TV. Too many cops on TV."

The inspector moved back to the man's alibi. He wanted the name of the man Raymond had worked for the night of the murder. Up to that point the answers had been coming easily enough, but for this he had to dig. Now Raymond wasn't certain of anything any more. Was that the night he had unloaded lettuce or was that the artichokes night? The way he was sweating out his answer, I began to think that his alibi wasn't going to hold up. The way I saw it, he was making a belated attempt to create something of a fog. In the end, he gave the inspector two names. If it was the lettuce night, then it would be Zimburg Brothers, or that was what he thought they were called. It was something like Zimburg. If it was the artichoke night, it would be someone called Kim.

"Kim," he said. "He's a Chink or a Jap. Kim, everybody up there they know him. He's the only one, he's in the market. A lot of them, they come up there to buy, but he's the only one up there selling."

I thought we'd be heading straight for the Bronx to check out the alibi. It was midmorning and the market activity by that time would have been hours in the past, but the offices of the wholesalers would still be open. They would be there, doing their paper work.

Back down in the street, however, Inspector Schmidt

picked up his car telephone. He was delegating the market check. One of his men would take care of that.

"No use wasting time up there," he said, as he was pulling away from the curb. "His alibi will check out."

"I thought you'd want to watch it checking out. He could have someone up there lying for him."

"And I'd see through it when one of my guys wouldn't?"

"I've known it to happen."

"You've known it to happen, kid, when I've seen through it and you didn't. Any one of my guys can handle this as well as I ever could. They wouldn't be on the squad if they couldn't."

"So where to now?"

"Mrs. Dutton. No matter how late she sleeps, she's got to be awake by now."

"Yes," I said, thinking aloud. "One thing sure is that Raymond didn't wear the stocking. It would stink of him if he had."

"Right, but there's the other sure thing. Dutton was the one who wore it. The lab tells us that."

"That sweat, sputum, and hair typing? I wonder how reliable that stuff is."

"The lab guys swear by it."

"It's crazy. What could he have been wearing it for and why would she lie about it?"

"If he was rehearsing for another hotel caper . . ."

"Why would she lie about that? What difference does it make now he's dead?"

"You're assuming she knew, and if she did, she could be worrying about his good name even after death."

"His good name? He didn't have too much of that."

"You know how she talks about him. He wasn't really a

crook; he was driven to it by a society that was too blind to give him his due."

"I would have thought she would tell me. We're good friends."

"And she didn't?"

"She didn't."

"So she wants his friends to think well of him—or she didn't know herself."

When we got down to the little house in the Village, she was not only awake, she was up and doing. It was much as it had been the night before. She was still at it, turning the house upside down, taking her inventory.

"I'm still going through things," she said, "but I don't think there's anything gone. If there is, it may be something that will mean a lot to me but not anything of monetary value." She fought down a sob. "It's all of him I have, things he touched, things he used, things he wore, things he liked."

"When we're through with it," the inspector said, "we'll get that pulled-out stocking with the eye holes in it back to you."

She shuddered.

"No," she said. "I never want to see that again."

"It's different from the other things he wore?"

"I don't understand."

"No," the inspector said. "I'm the one who doesn't understand. I'm counting on you to help me, Mrs. Dutton. The police laboratory says Harper Dutton was the one who wore it. The hair caught in it matches up to his hair. The spit dried on it matches up to his spit. The sweat is his sweat. Any one of the three would have been proof enough. All three, Mrs. Dutton?"

The color came high in her cheeks. She was blushing

furiously. With what looked like a painful effort she brought her gaze up to look us in the eye. She was summoning up her pride. She was not going to avoid facing us.

"I didn't want you to know," she said, "and now you're going to think it was because I was ashamed of it. It isn't that at all. It is just that it was so private. It belonged so much just to the two of us that I wanted to keep it to myself."

"I'm going to have to insist on your sharing it with me, Mrs. Dutton."

"I know. Of course, I must. You'll think it was perverted, kinky sex. Can you believe that it wasn't? It was sentimental. It was sweet."

"Dressing up? Re-enacting the night you met?"

"Not so much the first meeting but through all that time in the studio, the times we made love there. I was blindfolded with my arms strapped down to my sides."

"He had discarded the stocking mask by then."

"I know and I had seen his face, but behind my blindfold the stocking mask was in the image I had of him while we were making love. I know this must sound perverted, but it was an exciting look—phallic, I suppose."

"Let me get this straight, Mrs. Dutton. He put on the stocking mask and then he strapped your hands down at your sides and blindfolded you. This was before making love?"

"You mean in the studio or reconstructing it here?"

"Here. The night he was killed."

"Yes. That's the way it was."

"In the studio he wasn't masked."

"That's right."

"But he kept it on all the time you were making love."

That was a little more than she could take. Her pride gave out. She lowered her eyes. For the rest of it she talked without looking up at us.

"Yes."

"But you were blindfolded. You couldn't see."

"I could feel. It was his face against me, the feel of the nylon. Can you understand that it was something special, something that we had that was ours alone?"

"And before you fell asleep he took the mask off and freed your hands and took off your blindfold."

"Yes," she said. "The mask and the hands, but not the blindfold. We kept the blindfold on. It recreated the way we had been in the studio."

"In the studio your arms had been secured as well."

"I know, but staying that way through the night would have been a hardship, and he wouldn't do that to me. The blindfold was all right. Of course, you know now why I didn't see the man until just that glimpse of him as he went out of the window. I couldn't see him, not until I got the blindfold off. You should realize that this isn't easy for me, Inspector. That's why I lied to you about the stocking. I couldn't see where it could make any difference to you—and for that matter I still don't—but for me, it was protecting my privacy. I just know what the newspapers are going to make of it." She turned back to the inspector. "You will be giving it to the newspapers, won't you?"

"No," Schmitty said. "All the same, I can't promise that they won't have it. It will depend on how all this turns out. When we make an arrest and the DA gets an indictment, we'll know whether any of this has to be evidence in the case. In that event, of course, there will be testimony on it under oath, and I can't imagine that you'd want to perjure yourself."

"No," she said, "I wouldn't want to do that."

"I thought you wouldn't," the inspector said. "If it will be brought into court as part of the evidence, then it will be in the public record and there's nothing anyone can do about it. If it doesn't come out in court, then it's your business and there's no need to spread it around."

"I don't see how it could possibly be evidence," Jane said.

"Then you have nothing to worry about, Mrs. Dutton," Schmitty said.

VIII

Back at his Police Headquarters' desk, the inspector picked up the reports on the confirmation of William Raymond's alibi. It was solid for the beginning and for the end of the covered period, but it was peculiarly soft in between—so much so, in fact, that Schmitty changed his mind about leaving the confirmation process to his men. After reading their reports, he headed up to the Bronx and the produce market. I tagged along.

On the night of the killing Raymond had worked for a market man named Kim, a Korean. It is a fairly new manifestation in New York, but many Koreans have been coming into the fruit and vegetable business. They are mostly South Koreans, intellectuals and professionals unhappy with their government. Since language and other obstacles stand in the way of their practicing their professions in a foreign country, and since at home they had each been assiduous in the cultivation of a kitchen garden, dealing in produce has been for them a second area of expertise and one in which they can earn a living. For the most part, they have opened small neighborhood stores, but at the Hunts Point Market there was this one exception. Kim, possibly starting with more capital than

the others, had set up as a wholesaler, and he appeared
to be flourishing.

The inspector talked with Mr. Kim. He was a neat man
who presided over a neat office in which he kept neat records. He had a record of signing William Raymond on for
a night's work, and he had a record of paying him off in
the morning.

"I hired him," he said, "a little late. I like to have all
the men I need by eleven o'clock. I like to know I have
them before the trucks start coming in."

There was a noticeable accent in his English, but it was
more than serviceable.

"A little before eleven or a little after eleven is of no
consequence," Schmitty told him. "We're interested in a
later time."

"I understood that from the detectives who were here
before, but I want to explain something to you that I
should have explained to them. This Raymond, I don't
like taking him on unless I have to. It's only on a night
when I can't get as many people as I need. It's scraping
the bottom of the barrel, so I wait till the last possible
moment."

"Anything specific against him?"

The neat man had a neat list of complaints he had accumulated from his one experience of having hired William Raymond earlier in the week. It had been the first
night Raymond appeared in the market.

"The other men don't like him. They don't like working
with him. He's always looking for a fight."

It was said with the peace-loving man's contempt for
the bellicose.

"He's lazy, and he has a lazy man's dishonesty. He
doesn't give a full, honest night's work."

It was said with the industrious man's contempt for the indolent.

"He goofs off?"

"He signs on and he's there in the morning to collect his pay. Where he's been in between I can't say."

It didn't seem possible that anyone could have been running a business the way that sounded.

"You don't have a foreman or anyone to keep an eye on guys like this Raymond?" the inspector asked.

He tried to get along without hiring guys like Raymond, and he depended on the men he had on his regular payroll to keep the work going. Also, on his own sense of the flow of the crates, he could always have a good idea of whether the loading or unloading was going as quickly and as smoothly as it should.

"They're not going right," he said, "I step out to see what's wrong. The couple of nights I had Raymond on he stops for too many cigarettes or he walks off to the coffee stall too many times or he's gone off some place and he's taking a nap."

"The night before last?"

"Like the time before. He doesn't give an honest night's work."

"Missing for two hours or more?"

If you don't know the city, I better explain that. From the Hunts Point Market up in the Bronx to that little house in Greenwich Village near the lower end of Manhattan would be a long journey. The fastest way of doing it would be by subway, and a man would have to hit on the luckiest sort of conditions if he was to do the round trip in anything more than a few minutes under two hours.

"I hope not," Kim said. "I know the man cheats. I'd hate to think he could cheat me that much."

"He wasn't working alone. The other men?"

"They say he's always goofing off."

"Two hours or more?"

"I've asked them. They won't say yes and they won't say no."

"They knew it was the police who were asking?"

"They know. Want to know what I think, Inspector?"

"Any ideas you have, Mr. Kim."

"I don't think he could have been gone for anything like two hours. I just don't think it's possible without my knowing it. I also have a feeling about the men."

"And that is?"

"Raymond's not a likable man. Everybody hates him. I think if they could tell the police that he was away for the time you're asking about, they would have jumped at the chance. They would enjoy it to see him in trouble. They go as far as they can to make trouble for him. I think they could tell you he was away from the loading platform a lot, but it would be ten minutes here, a quarter of an hour there, maybe a half hour another time. They complain to me about that. As much as two hours, they would have told me. They would have told me not to pay him."

"He's tough and big and mean," the inspector said. "Maybe they're afraid of him."

"Little, weak men don't work up here in the market, Inspector. He's big and tough, but I've got a couple that are bigger and tougher. Maybe they're not meaner, but they are bigger and tougher."

And that was the picture. It came close to corroboration of Raymond's alibi, but it wasn't conclusive. There was, of course, another possibility—that Kim was misjudging his men. He rejected outright any suggestion that they could have been coerced or seduced or even bought into lying for him.

"He's not a man who makes friends," he kept saying. "He's a man who makes enemies."

Immediately after the killing Inspector Schmidt had ordered a check not only on Raymond but on the other four as well, the whole crew that had been with Dutt on the Sandringham job. The reports had been coming in. Three of them were easy: Stevens, Carlson, and Peters were well fixed for alibis. All three of them were in jail. While Harper Dutton had been out of circulation, those three had been doing singles acts, and without the Dutton planning and execution, none of the three had been up to it. It had been three clumsy jobs, three easy arrests, and three juries that hadn't been able to find anything that approached a reasonable doubt.

All three had left the city and had committed their crimes in the jurisdictions of other states. The jails that had them in residence, therefore, were all far west of the Hudson, and in those jails all three were accounted for. They had been missing no head counts. Those three, accordingly, Inspector Schmidt could write off. Only Cal Gibbons of the Sandringham gang was at large and unaccounted for.

"It would be that bastard," I said.

Schmitty grinned at me.

"And, if he's evening scores, maybe you better be watching out."

"Me? Why me?"

"Gibbons? He's the one who was with you in the car, wasn't he? He's the one who had the gun on Dutton back then. As I remember it, all three of you—Mrs. Gordon,

Mrs. Dutton, and you—were convinced that he would have killed Dutton if you hadn't been there to chop him down. Actually, all four of you were agreed on that, Dutton, too. Gibbons came that close to massacring the four of you. He was the one, wasn't he?"

"But that was to keep us from blowing their game, Schmitty. What makes you think he'd come after me now?"

"He owes you for that one good chop."

"He was acquitted."

"Let's not forget the Sandringham loot, Baggy. If Gibbons was done out of his share and he killed Dutton, he could be holding you responsible as well. After all, if you hadn't chopped him at that crucial moment in the car, he wouldn't have been done out of his share, and with Dutton dead, it would have been a better split. He's got a lot to hold against you."

"You trying to scare me?"

"Just trying to persuade you to be careful. Watch yourself."

"Okay," I said. "Until you have this thing cleaned up, I won't leave your side. I won't be out of your sight."

It was another twenty-four hours before the word came in on Cal Gibbons. He was not only on the loose, he had never left town. He was in the city, and the inspector's boys had located him. He was living in a hotel on upper Broadway. From the address it had to be a good mile north of that stretch that the building of Lincoln Center has boosted toward regeneration.

From the address I knew everything that anybody would need to know. The hotels in that area had never been de luxe, but in their day they had been decent, middle-class residences. The neighborhood around them had done a slide into slum, and the residents, frightened by what they saw in the streets, had moved away to areas where they felt less threatened.

The hotels weren't left standing empty. They filled up again, but lots of the new residents were zonked out in hopeless poverty. These were the welfare clients, people who had been born on public assistance, grown up on it, were living their lives on it, and had no expectations but that they would die on it.

Others were zonked out on the sedatives prescribed for them when the overcrowded mental hospitals judged them to have a chance of making it on the outside, but only in a semi-stupor that would keep them from being a danger to themselves or to the community. The hospitals, accordingly, put them out on their own to nod away their days because the hospital space was needed.

Obviously, Cal Gibbons, as I had known him, fitted into neither of these categories; but I could visualize him as a wolf roaming loose in the zonked-out sheepfold. There would be relief checks and Social Security checks to be ripped off. It was a good location for a pusher. For a tough crook one of those hotels could be the land of opportunity, and I knew Cal Gibbons to be a tough crook.

His hotel, when we got up there, ran true to form. There was a man in the lobby, and he was talking to himself. It was an easy assumption that in his right mind he wouldn't be talking to himself since—from what he was saying, it was obvious that he didn't like himself. There were the people with the bulging paper shopping bags. There were the people who had the lost look that comes of seeing through eyes where the pupils are contracted down to the size of a pinhead.

There was a young black man in a dirty T-shirt that

said across his chest: "Kiss me I'm Aryan." On the back of
the shirt was something unprintable anywhere but on the
back of a dirty T-shirt. He sat in the lobby, nodding with
the rest, and when Inspector Schmidt looked at him, he
didn't look at the inspector. He just went on nodding. The
inspector looked away. He took my arm and propelled me
toward the elevator.

"Okay," he said. "Our guy's still upstairs. He hasn't
moved. We'll go up."

"How do you know he's still up there?" I asked.

I knew that the boys had only located Gibbons. They
were leaving him for the inspector to have first crack at
him.

"If there'd been any change and he had to tell me
what, he'd have stopped nodding to shake his head like
he thought he had a fly crawling across his forehead."

"Who?"

"The Aryan."

"He's yours?"

"Yeah. He's new and good. You don't know him yet."

"I like his T-shirt."

"So does he. He says police work gets monotonous if
you do it without laughs."

"But he can't see his own back."

"He remembers it from when he puts the shirt on. He's
got a good memory."

"From when he put it on? That looks like a month ago
and never washed since."

"If he's staking out the Waldorf, he cleans up."

We were in the elevator and on our way up, but it was
a slow ride, a creeping ascent punctuated with what felt
like hiccuping hesitations of the mechanism. It could
have been that it was paced to give a passenger ample

time for reading all the graffiti scratched into the paneling of the car. I read them. I always read graffiti although it's only occasionally that you come on any that says something new or says the old stuff differently. This wasn't one of those occasions. That car was a temple of cloacal cliché.

It took us up to six and we looked for 631. We found a door where the nailed-on tin numbers read 931. The 6, unmoored from its upper nail, was hanging upside down.

Inspector Schmidt knocked. The response was quick. A woman opened the door. She was all smiles; but, at sight of us, the smile shrunk to a sulky pout. She had frizzy hair that looked like iron shavings badly gone to rust. The shiny blue of her tight, sleazy dress was an act of aggression. It was a color that stabbed your eyes. Her breasts and her buttocks were also acts of aggression. They looked as though they were armor plated under the shiny rayon.

"I thought you was the guy bringing the bottle," she said.

"Sorry. We're not the guy bringing the bottle," Schmitty said. "Cal Gibbons here?"

"Who wants him?"

"We do."

"Who are you? Friends of his?"

The inspector indicated me.

"My buddy here knew him once."

"He's asleep."

"He wakes. He'll want to wake for the bottle."

"The bottle's for me."

"Okay. Then he'll wake for us."

"I don't know."

"We know."

"How do you know?"

"Because we're police."

She moved to shut the door in our faces, but it would take a lot more than she had to do that to the inspector. He stood his ground and the door stayed open.

"He don't tell me nothing about what he does nights. I don't know nothing."

"I haven't asked you anything," Schmitty said. "I haven't yet."

"They's nothing to ask."

"You want to wake him or do I do it?"

She retreated into the room. We followed after her. The inspector pushed the door shut behind us. It was a one-room-kitchenette-and-bath job. You could stand just inside the door and see all of it. The bathroom door stood ajar, and the whole of it was in sight. There were some stockings hung over the tub and a couple of handkerchiefs were stretched over the wall tiles to dry.

The kitchenette was just an open alcove. The tap of the kitchen sink was dripping and there was a stain in the sink that said it had been a long time since the washer first needed replacing. The room had a fold-away sofa-bed. It was unfolded and Gibbons lay sleeping on it. At least I was assuming it was he. He was sprawled bottoms up. We couldn't see his face. Except for an undershirt he was naked.

The woman walked over to the bed. Her walk had that undulating eloquence, or it would have had if the armor hadn't been so forbidding. She stood for a moment looking down on the man on the bed. Then she whacked him on the rump.

He mumbled a protest, but he didn't move.

"Wake up," she said. "You got visitors."

"What visitors?"

"Cop visitors. That's what."

"That ain't funny."

"If it ain't funny, you ain't got to laugh. They ain't laughing."

That he wasn't laughing was obvious. At the word cop all the ease had gone out of him. He wasn't moving, but he was now lying there tense. He had made the perceptible shift from true indolence to what was only a pretense of indolence. He was playing for time, taking some moments to think and to plan. We waited while he went through an elaborate ritual of simulated waking. He yawned. He stretched. He carried through on the whole performance without once turning his head. He was not letting us see his face until he would have it composed in the expression he was choosing to present to us.

Eventually he was ready. He turned and looked at us. His eyes fastened on me and I had an astonishing effect on him. He relaxed. He grinned. All the tension went out of him.

"Give me a sec," he said. "I'll just get me some pants on."

The girl had been edging toward the door. As though this move he was making toward clothing his nakedness might be her signal to depart, she reached for the doorknob.

"I'll be going now," she said.

"Don't go," he said. "They won't be staying long."

Now he had gone tense again. His words were more a command than a request. You could have thought that he was afraid that if she went out the door, he would never see her again and that it would be a loss he couldn't endure.

With all too evident reluctance she came away from the door. It was obvious that she didn't want to stay, but she'd had her orders. It also seemed obvious that he was used to being obeyed. I was guessing that he had her well drilled in a habit of obedience. She hung near the door as though poised for flight, but she wasn't moving.

While Gibbons was pulling on his pants, Inspector Schmidt was reading him his rights. He took them with a derisive grin. It was a good guess that he'd had them read to him so many times before that he might be letter perfect in them. His demeanor was making it plain that they bored him.

Jerking his zipper closed, he broke in on the inspector.

"You don't need all of that," he said, "unless you're going to pull me in for screwing."

Ignoring the interruption, Schmitty went on through the last of the required words.

"You say that real nice," Gibbons told him.

"How's for you to talk real nice?"

"How's for you showing me some ID, and how's for you telling me what you want to know?"

Schmitty brought out the ID.

"Inspector?" Gibbons said. "Big shot. How come I rate it?"

"I ask the questions. You give the answers."

"So ask."

The man was cocky, and I couldn't believe he was putting on an act. I had seen him tense up. It had been too clearly visible. So I knew he wasn't that good at dissembling. Something had taken the tension out of him. He couldn't have been more at ease. There was no play acting in it.

"What do you do nights?"

"One night it's one thing. Another night it's another. Name a night."

The inspector named it.

Gibbons turned to the girl.

"You tell him, baby," he said. "What did I do that night, and how did you like it?"

"We ate in the Chink joint next block down Broadway. We went across the street to the movies."

"After the movies?"

"We came up here."

"For how long?"

"Till morning. Eleven o'clock, twelve o'clock. We got up late."

"He was here all that time? He didn't go out for a while and come back?"

"All the time. People, they've got to sleep some time."

"You slept?"

"We slept."

Gibbons leered at her.

"And done other things," he said.

Passing that by, Schmitty persisted with the girl.

"You slept," he said. "How do you know he didn't go out for a while during the time you were asleep."

She giggled.

"It's him sleeps like that, like a rock, not me. You seen just now how I had to wake him."

"You're a light sleeper?"

"Anything'll wake me. Guys, they're one way; girls, they're different. They're all like that. It's how so many johns—girls rob them. Guys go out like a light; gals lay awake and watch them sleep. When we do go off, it's just sleep and wake, sleep and wake. Anything moves, it wakes me up."

"It's the night that Dutton guy got his. It's that night you're asking about," Gibbons said.

"So?"

"So that other guy, the one called Raymond, he's out."

"He works nights. He was way up in the Bronx at work."

Gibbons laughed.

"And I play nights," he said. "I was up here playing."

"Just that one night," Schmitty said. "Not every night."

"Lots of nights but not every night. Nobody can get it made every night, not even me."

There was a knock at the door. It was the guy with the bottle. The girl took it from him and told him to keep the change. He had the lobotomized look of one of the sedated schizos. He took off and the girl opened the bottle. She took a quick drag on it and then went to the kitchenette alcove and fussed around looking for washed glasses. There weren't any. She gave a couple a quick rinse. I could see that it wasn't enough of a rinse to get rid of the lipstick smears.

She turned to us. Hospitality had set in. She was playing the hostess.

"Snort?" she offered.

"Not on duty," Schmitty said. "Thanks, no."

She took that to mean the both of us. I was satisfied to leave it at that. It wasn't my brand.

She passed the bottle to Gibbons. He didn't refuse it, but he'd only barely wet his lips with it before he handed it back to her. She gave him a questioning look, but then she shrugged. She wasn't taxing herself with trying to understand the incomprehensible. She was shrugging it off. She started the bottle back to her lips, but before she had it up there, the inspector reached over and took it out of her hand. She relinquished it gracefully.

"I'll get you a glass," she said, starting toward the kitchenette.

"No," the inspector said. "Don't bother. It's just to put off your getting sloshed until after we're through here."

That she didn't like. She reached for the bottle.

"You got no right," she said.

"We won't be long. We'll be through soon," Schmitty promised.

"You're through right now," Gibbons said. "Not the one, Raymond, so one of them other guys was to the hotel with him."

"They're all in the slammer."

Gibbons grinned.

"So you got them," he said. "Me? You can't touch me. I got an alibi."

"Theirs are better," Schmitty said. "That night they were already in."

"So he had other guys hating his guts."

"Who?"

"How do I know who?"

"You brought them up."

"Look, Inspector. He was a snotty bastard. There wasn't a guy who knowed him wasn't itching to kick his ass. The thing was he was smart. He knew how to operate. It wasn't just he had big ideas. He had the way of making them work. Fellows go in with a guy like that. It ain't because they like him. It's just they got to hold still for him."

"Until you get ready to bump him," Schmitty said.

Gibbons looked at me and from me back to the inspector.

"His story," he said, indicating me. "In case you don't know, the jury didn't believe him. They believed me. I wasn't even there."

"I know," the inspector said. "The jury believed him all right. They just weren't sure enough you were the one."

"That's right. I was never there. So what do you want from me?"

"You said he had other enemies."

Gibbons grinned. "Like the guys they was with him on the hotel job," he said. "We wasn't, none of us except that Raymond. We was on trial for that job and we was acquitted. So that's all washed out. You know it's all washed out."

"And since it is, you can talk and not worry. You can't be tried for the Sandringham job again."

"I can't be tried for anything. I got an alibi."

"And Dutton had enemies. Who?"

"Look. On that hotel job he fixes it so it's too dangerous to be around him, and all the time he's building it to get rid of them other guys before the split. So it's the guys was with him and Raymond that night at the hotel, or maybe it's even other guys. Was the hotel job the only time? A guy like him, he's got enemies like a cat's got kittens. They come natural."

The inspector offered the girl the bottle. She snatched it out of his hand.

"That's it," he said. "You can start living it up now."

I waited till we were out on Broadway before I asked my question.

"How good is his alibi?"

"As good as Raymond's."

I couldn't buy that.

"If Raymond's is phony, he has a whole army of people

lying for him and for no reason. Gibbons has nobody but that babe, and she could have good reasons."

"Weren't you watching?" Schmitty asked. "Didn't you see?"

"What should I have seen?"

"First of all, the girl. She wasn't going down any road for him."

"You mean she said she didn't know what he did nights? When you pinned the night down, she contradicted herself."

"Not necessarily a contradiction. I read it the other way. She doesn't want any trouble. A night he's not with her, she has a good idea of what he's doing. It's night work. Muggings? Burglary? Or is he always doing himself that much good in some crap game? If she doesn't know it's not a crap game, she has her suspicions, and so far as she's concerned, he's on his own. She's not going to lie for him. All she was telling me was that she doesn't have any part of what he does when he's not with her. Since I picked on a night when he was with her, she could answer for that and she did."

"Possible," I said, "but when did you begin getting so trusting?"

"Watching him. That's when I began."

He'd seen nothing I hadn't seen; but, where I had merely observed, he had understood. First there had been the impossibly slow awakening.

"He wasn't asleep. He was lying doggo and thinking fast."

"I recognized that. So why if he had nothing to think about?"

"He had plenty to think about, all those nights for which she wouldn't alibi him. Those nights were worrying him. When he turned to face us, he was braced for questions about those nights, but then all of a sudden he was as relaxed as a rug and couldn't have been cockier."

"I saw that, too, and I still don't get it."

"You have to ask what relaxed him."

"Okay," I said. "I'm asking."

"You," Schmitty told me. "It was the sight of you that told him he was all right. Seeing you, he knew what we'd come for, and he began enjoying what for him must have been a wonderful new experience. He was innocent. He had nothing to hide and, if I wasn't going to believe him, he had the girl to give him an alibi and the best kind, the simple truth."

"So where are we? Do we go looking for an unknown who was with Dutton on some other caper we know nothing about?"

"Not me," Schmitty said. "I don't go messing around with the unknown, not while I still have the known to work on."

"But you've just been convincing me that you're fresh out of anything to work on. Raymond is alibied for the night of the killing and so is Gibbons. The other three have the most unassailable alibis. What's left?"

"The timing, that's what's left. Revenge waits for years, and then within a week after Raymond comes out, the waiting stops. Are we going to call that a coincidence?"

"What else can you call it as long as you can't break through Raymond's alibi?"

"I'm calling it an indication," the inspector said.

"An indication of what?"

"An indication of what goes on. I'm leaving Allen where he is."

"Who's Allen?"

"Joe Allen, the Aryan."

"But it's Raymond who was out less than a week."

"He's staked out, too. He has been ever since we first found him. Now we wait till the fellows tell us they're moving."

IX

The word didn't come through until that night, and even then it was not till well after midnight. In the interim Inspector Schmidt kept busy. The only thing I could make of all his activity was that behind the facade of satisfied confidence he was presenting to me he was less certain than he pretended to be.

He spent all the time going back to the beginning of things. He ordered up the department files on the Sandringham Hotel job and the ensuing kidnap. They were voluminous files. He had his shoes off and, with his feet propped up on his desk, he worked on the files all day and all evening. From time to time he would be interrupted by reports from his two stakeouts. The boys were keeping him informed on all movements made by Raymond and Gibbons. The inspector kept a chart of their movements, but it was obvious to me that he was only being methodical. Nothing he was getting from those quarters was turning him on.

He wasn't reading everything in that great pile of stuff he'd had pulled from the files. It would have taken days, if not weeks, to read it all. For at least a couple of hours he was just flipping through, separating out from the mass those specific items he would read and study.

When it came time for lunch, he sent out for it and we ate at his desk. At dinner time we did it again. Between times there were containers of coffee and some of the time coffee and. Long before the break came I was unable to put my mind to much of anything but speculation on how long it might take before a man would come down with a galloping case of sandwich-doughnut-and-coffee poisoning.

All through I'd been reading along after the inspector. I might have been able to divert myself with the reading, but it was all too familiar. I had been over it too many times. I had made my statement about it, and I had testified to it. I had seen the statements made by Alexandra and Jane. I'd heard Alexandra testify. I had talked about it with Alexandra and later with Jane. Early and late I had talked about it with Inspector Schmidt.

That part of what he was poring over was dull only through overfamiliarity. The other items he was studying were just dull. They were the lists of what had been lost out of those safe-deposit boxes, the Police Department lists, and the insurance company lists. There were the lists of the people who had put in claims—names, addresses, Sandringham room numbers. There were the lists of stolen jewelry, stolen papers, stolen cash.

I tried to read all that junk. I tried to be as interested in it as Inspector Schmidt appeared to be, but trying wasn't enough. I kept nodding. Then I'd jerk awake and find myself with no idea of how far I'd read. In the course of the evening it got worse. I'd doze off and come awake catching myself as I was about to fall out of my chair. About midevening I gave up on it. There is a sofa in the inspector's office. I've never known him to use it. I don't know what he has it in there for unless it is as an accommodation for me.

I repaired to it and had a try at reading those files lying down. Of course, I went right off to sleep. It was better than the chair—no chance of falling. There was, however, also no nodding into overbalance that would serve to wake me up. I just corked off and had a good, long, restful nap.

I expected I'd be wakened from it by the inspector when he would set up a great and joyful shout of "Eureka." I'd been waiting for some such all through those hours in his office, but no shout came. It must be assumed that Inspector Schmidt is a more silent and restrained man than was Archimedes.

When he did wake me, I knew at once that it was not because he'd failed to find what he'd been seeking that there had been no cry of "Eureka." He was looking too well-satisfied. His was not the look of failure.

"Time to go," he said, shaking me awake.

While Schmitty was climbing into his shoes, I had a moment or two for pulling myself together and yawning the sleep out of my eyes. The shoes are the infallible signal. You know about the inspector's area of weakness: His feet have never recovered from the punishment they took way back when he was a beat-pounding rookie. He goes shod only when he must.

"Found something?" I asked.

I was trying to imagine what it could be. Certainly there could be nothing in that ancient history that could have served to poke a hole in either Raymond's or Gibbons' alibi.

"As much as I'll ever find on paper," Schmitty said. "I just had a call from the Aryan. They're moving."

"They? Gibbons and his babe?"

"The babe? She doesn't know what he does with his nights unless it's a night when he's doing her."

"Then Gibbons and who?"

"Gibbons and Raymond, joint action."

"They got together?"

"And they're moving together. Come on, Baggy, get the lead out."

He was starting out the door. I followed after him.

"Moving where?" I asked.

"They never had the guts to move against Dutton. Or maybe just that once for Gibbons—that night in the car. Dutton was too much for them. They knew that. He'd given them too powerful a demonstration of it. Now, with Dutton out of the way, they're figuring Mrs. Dutton will be less formidable. They're expecting they'll be able to handle her."

"Jane? That's crazy. All right. I can see where Gibbons might have it in for me. I did spoil his play that night in the car, but Jane? She was victim all the way. What can they have against her?"

"Their kind never forgets. She was Dutton's wife."

"Him and his? Oh, come on, Schmitty. If he was alive, they could try to get at him through her, but the man's dead. You telling me that he's looking down from someplace up there or looking up from someplace in the fire and brimstone, and he'll see what they're doing and it'll make him suffer?"

"They're not interested in his suffering. All they care about is their own pleasure and profit."

I'd been wondering about what the inspector could

have found in the files. If this was any indication, it seemed idiotic. They did contain my account of the sadistic pranks Raymond played on me during that day in the studio. They also contained reasonably convincing indications that Gibbons, unleashed, might well be another of the same breed. But the inspector had known about all that. I couldn't imagine that he would have needed all those hours for mulling it over.

Down in Police Plaza the inspector's car was out of the garage and waiting for him with the motor running. He whipped it out past the Municipal Building. Short of old Boss Tweed's courthouse he turned north. While he drove, he was getting running reports on his car radiophone.

Having joined forces at Gibbons' hotel, Gibbons and Raymond, followed by the Aryan and the man Schmitty'd had staked out on Raymond, were headed downtown. From where they were starting, up in the West Nineties, it was a far longer run down to the little house in the Village than the trip we were making up from Police Headquarters.

They hadn't started on wheels. It had taken them some time before they could steal a car. We were having the reports. They had gotten that made, and they were on their way downtown. Schmitty seemed to be doubting not even for a moment that their target would be Jane Dutton. For a man who was just riding a hunch, he seemed to be far too confident.

"The boys overheard something?" I asked.

"No. They can't come that close without blowing their tail. It's only what they're seeing."

"Then how can you be so sure they're headed for Jane's?"

"Where else would they be headed?"

"Millions of places. They got together to pull a job. There are all sorts of possibilities—all the midtown hotels and banks—anything from some neighborhood branch to the Federal Reserve. There's Tiffany. There's Cartier. There's Winston. This is a big town, and it's stuffed with places that have loot in them."

"Within three days of the time when Dutton was knocked off? Explain the timing."

I tried.

"Let's say Dutt was the one who got away with the whole of the Sandringham take," I began.

"Yes," Schmitty said. "Let's say that."

"As long as he was alive, they maybe had some hope that there would still be a split, that they would work it out with him some way. Now that he's dead, that would be a hope gone glimmering. So now they've written the Sandringham do off as the dead past, and they're living in the present and for the future. They're going to do another job. What's wrong with that timing?"

"What's wrong with a job on Jane Dutton, his widow and his heiress?"

"There's not even any certainty that they're out to do a job tonight. They could even have gotten together just for the preliminaries, casing the place they want to hit."

"They don't steal a car just to go downtown to case a joint. They're not joyride-hungry teenies."

There he had something I had to concede.

"All right," I said. "They're doing the job tonight, but you're thinking it's a lead-pipe cinch they're after Jane. I can't buy it, Schmitty, not all of it, not on the little you've got."

"You think they'd just let go that easy? Leave her to sit fat with all the loot?"

"She hasn't got it," I protested. "She's never had it. She would have turned it in."

"They don't know her the way you do, Baggy."

It was only with that answer that the inspector made any start on having me believe. In such experience as I'd had of the two men, I had been anything but impressed with their intelligence or their wisdom. Neither of them had ever drawn an honest breath or carried an honest thought in his head. From what I knew about crooks, I could well imagine that their thinking would run to the assumption that they were no different from the rest of mankind. Since they were dishonest, they would be convinced that everyone else was dishonest and that people, generally believed to be honest, were only people who had been successful in preserving a false front. Obviously, there could be no common ground between them and me in our opinions of Jane Harcourt Dutton.

We rolled into her street. The little house was ablaze with light from top to bottom. There was going to be no need for waking Jane. That was understandable. After what she had been through, anyone would have trouble sleeping. Even in ordinary times she had an insomnia problem—in fact, if it hadn't been for her insomnia, we would never have met.

Driving past the house, the inspector turned the corner and found a parking spot on the avenue.

"It'll only be a little while now," he said. "We'll do without progress reports. I don't want them spotting my parked car and getting scared off."

"If they're headed somewhere else," I said, "you'll have no way of knowing."

"If they're headed somewhere else," Schmitty said, "I won't be interested."

We walked back to the house. There was no immediate response to the inspector's ring. I saw a curtain move at one of the windows, but then it was only a few moments before Jane opened the door. She greeted us with an apology. A ring that time of night—obviously she wouldn't be answering before she knew who it was.

She was dressed—slacks and a blouse, her hair done up in a scarf, bedroom slippers.

"You have news for me?" she asked.

"I need your co-operation," the inspector told her. "We haven't much time. Raymond and Gibbons, you remember them?"

"How could I forget?"

That her tone was bitter was at least understandable.

"They've joined forces, and they're headed this way. They'll be here in a few minutes. We'll be waiting for them with you, but we'll be in the back room. I'd like you to douse all your lights and undress and get into bed. I want them to think they're catching you unprepared."

"What can they want here now?" she asked.

"They'll want to deal with you."

"Deal with me? For what?"

"A split on what your husband took out of the Sandringham that night."

"But they're the ones who got it. Dutt didn't get any of it."

"In that case," Schmitty said, "Raymond and Gibbons won't be coming here. We'll wait and see. Meanwhile, Mrs. Dutton, please, your clothes off and get into bed. We'll be turning the lights off meanwhile, but we have to move. We have only minutes."

She shuddered.

"If they are coming here," she said, "they're coming to kill me. What good will you be to me if you're in the next room? I'll have witnesses? So what? I'll be dead."

"Why should they kill you, Mrs. Dutton?"

"Because they're animals, that's why. They're savages. Why should they have killed Dutt?"

"They can be thinking you'll be easier to deal with," Schmitty said.

She moved off into her bedroom. She left the door slightly ajar so that she could talk through the opening while behind the door she was changing.

"But they must know that there's nothing to deal," she argued.

"Not necessarily. There were the three others in on the thing that night. It could have been that in the confusion one of them got away with the stuff, and these two don't know it. They think it was your husband. Since he was the leader and since, even when things were breaking down, he was the one who was in command of the situation, you can see how they would think that way."

She laughed. I was dashing about the place hitting light switches. I recognized that laugh of hers. This was the woman who had chosen for herself the life of stimulation and excitement. I was thinking of all that chitchat between her and Alexandra while we were being held in the bar at the Sandringham. I was thinking that none of us could have imagined even then that she was going to find this much excitement. I couldn't speak for stimulation, but it seemed a good guess that there had been that as well.

"If you're wrong, Inspector," she said, "I'll come back

to haunt you. Don't you think I won't. My ghost will be with you always. It won't give you a moment's peace."

The inspector laughed with her.

"If I ever made that kind of a mistake," he said, "it sure would haunt me. Your ghost could spare itself the trouble."

"Whatever comes of this, even if it's nothing," she said, "I'm glad the two of you came. It will help me get through the night. Last night was dreadful. I couldn't sleep a wink. It was enough to show me. I'll never be able to sleep in this house again. Tonight I haven't even been trying. I've been packing. I packed all day and I was going to pack straight through the night. Tomorrow I'm getting out of here. I thought I'd want to stay because it's here that I have all my memories of Dutt, but it won't work. There's the one memory that wipes out all the others. I keep seeing the man in the window and Dutt dead in the bed beside me. I'm taking all his things with me, but I have to get away from this room, the bed, the window."

"You still haven't put bars on the window," I said.

"The next people who'll live here can do that. I'm through with this place."

"Where are you planning on going?"

"Abroad." She choked up for a moment, but she quickly brought herself back under control. "I wanted to go with Dutt," she said. "If we could have gone, he'd be alive now . . ."

The inspector broke in and shushed her. He wanted them to come to what would seem like a sleeping house, dark and silent.

We sat in the dark and waited. With every minute that passed I was the more convinced that we were out on a wild goose chase, that uncharacteristically the inspector had staked everything on a bad hunch. I was trying to calculate relative times. There was our short run against their far-longer trip. There was the lead we'd had on them during the time they were walking the streets in search of a car they could steal. There was the speed of Inspector Schmidt's driving. Against it there was the assumption that they would be driving at a circumspect pace and would be exercising the greatest care to observe all red lights and to obey every traffic regulation. Only the silliest of juvenile delinquents invites arrest for speeding while he's driving a stolen car.

I was making all these allowances, but I still had the feeling that the time was stretching too long and that Inspector Schmidt had made the wrong guess. I should have known better. Just as I was about to share this thinking of mine with the inspector, I heard a car pull up in front of the house.

Straining, I could hear the sound of the doors opening and shutting. Nothing came through but small clicks, the stealthy sound of car doors eased open, car doors eased shut.

I was still so far from being convinced, however, that I was telling myself that what might seem like stealth could just as readily be nothing more than well-bred consideration. A neighbor has been out late. He drives into the sleeping street, taking care lest he disturb the slumbers of the good householders in their beds. He might even be an erring husband hoping to sneak in without alerting his wife.

But then I was hearing small clicks of another sort. These were sharper and they were closer. They came from the street door. The well-bred, considerate neighbor or even the erring husband wouldn't be at work on the lock in the front door of a house that wasn't his. He doesn't pick locks, and he doesn't fiddle around trying for a master that will work.

The door swung open. It had a hinge that could have taken a little oil. Floor boards creaked. This was an old house; its original floors preserved. Then there was a brief interval of no sound, but the creaks picked up again and this time they came from the bedroom.

I wondered how they could know the house so well that they had been able to zero in on the bedroom so unerringly, moving in the dark straight to their objective without a moment of hesitation or the smallest wrong turn. I was asking myself if it was possible that they had been there before, perhaps to see Dutt. Gibbons, after all, had been at large all along, and even Raymond, although he had been out only the few days, might in the course of those few days have been there to visit.

I couldn't believe that any such thing could have occurred without its troubling Jane, and I would have expected that she would have come to me with her trouble. We had, after all, during the years of Dutt's imprisonment, developed that sort of relationship. It was still a possibility, however, if they had come at a time when she might have been out of the house. I tried to think back over what I knew of the pattern of their lives together. It seemed to me that there would have been plenty of times when she was in the house alone while Dutt was off at work in the gallery. I couldn't visualize any occasion when she might have been out and he alone in the house.

She had always been most careful to schedule for his working hours any of the things she did without him—visits to the hairdresser, shopping trips. I had often thought that it was all she could do to make herself stay away from the gallery and leave him alone there to do his job.

But then I remembered. These had been thin days for news. The papers had gone to town with the Harper Dutton killing. I had seen the page-one drawings of the floor plan of the house. They had been complete, even to the exact placement of the furniture. There was nothing to say that Gibbons and Raymond weren't newspaper readers; but, even if they weren't, it wouldn't have been beyond them to look at the pictures without moving their lips.

This may have been a lot of thinking for me to have been doing in what was no more than a matter of seconds, but that sort of thinking goes quickly. It's not the kind you slog away at. The thoughts come unbidden and they just whiz through your mind. When you are concentrated on listening and you're not stopping to examine them, the thoughts whiz even faster.

The next sound was sharp and unmistakable. It was the rattling descent of a Venetian blind. Nobody passing along the street, if there should be someone at that hour, was to be given any opportunity of seeing in. It was immediately followed by a show of light in that crack of the door where Jane had left it slightly ajar.

Jane gave out with a small, strangled yelp.

"Don't scream, baby. Nobody's going to hurt you. You play fair with us. We'll play fair with you. So let's talk."

It was Gibbons' voice.

"Nobody's going to hurt you," Raymond added, "unless it's you want to be hurt."

"Who are you? What do you want?"

For a moment I thought she was giving it the wrong

play, pretending that she didn't know them; but then I remembered that she had skipped out before the trial, so much before, in fact, that she had been gone before any of them had been picked up. Alexandra and I had been the ones who'd seen them day after day in the courtroom; Jane had not.

"Hubby's old buddies," Raymond said.

"We want our split. What do you think we want?"

That was Gibbons.

"Split of what?"

"What we took out of the Sandringham that night. What else?"

"You had it all. You, or the others. The lot of you saw to that. Dutt never had a penny of it. If he had, he'd have given it back. He wasn't like you. He'd made his mistake, and he had learned his lesson. He wasn't going to make another."

"Nice house," Gibbons said. "Nice things. All you got here, it costs. Who do you think you're kidding?"

"We're wasting time," Raymond said. "Look at this place. She's been packing up. She's getting ready to skip."

"Don't be ridiculous," Jane told him. "My husband was killed in this house, right here in this room three nights ago. I don't know which one of you did it. It was probably both of you and all for nothing. You came to the wrong place. There are those three others. Go to them."

"We're wasting time, Cal," Raymond said.

"Comes to look like it," Gibbons agreed.

There was the sound of a light slap. I started for the bedroom door. The inspector grabbed at my arm and held me back.

"No good your trying to yell," Gibbons said. "Nothing anybody'll hear is going to come through his hand."

That explained the sound. Raymond had slapped his hand down over her mouth and he was holding it there. She couldn't scream. Gibbons went on talking and his tone woke echoes for me. It was the tone he had used when he was holding his gun on us in the Sandringham bar.

"We're going to gag you, and we're going to tape your mouth shut over the gag. Then we're going to tie you up. That's when we start hurting you, baby. How much we've got to hurt you, that's going to depend on you. You want to be stubborn, we can hurt you a lot. Long and slow is the way we'll do it. Or else we don't have to hurt you at all. We're not asking for anything it ain't ours. We're not asking for nothing but you treat us fair and square. A sixth for him and a sixth for me. That ain't much. It leaves you with more than what's your right. It leaves you with two-thirds, and it'll be yours to keep, yours anyhow till the other guys maybe catch up with you. The way you and hubby been doing us, by rights we hadn't ought to leave you have anything, but you're a widow woman."

"Yeah," Raymond added, "and we're soft about widow women. If they behaves theirselves, we're soft on them."

That declaration was followed by lengthening moments of silence. They seemed to be waiting for Jane to give them some answer, but she couldn't speak with Raymond's big paw heavy on her mouth and, if he lifted it even slightly, they would be running the risk of her screaming. They couldn't know that she had no need to scream. I had to guess that they were waiting for her to give them some sort of sign. Whether she gave them none or whether it was a signal that didn't satisfy them we had no way of knowing. When Gibbons spoke again, however, it was evident that it had been one or the other.

"I guess you're one of them, they wants to be hurt," he said. "Maybe you think it's going to be kicks."

That did it. Inspector Schmidt moved. He kicked the bedroom door wide, and he planted himself in the doorway with his gun at the ready.

"Don't give them a thing, Mrs. Dutton," he said. "They have nothing coming to them from you. They don't deserve anything from you. They're too stupid. You can leave them to me. I'll see that they get what they have coming to them."

Gibbons was sputtering. Raymond was saying nothing, but he pulled his hand away from Jane's mouth and stepped away from the bed. The inspector spoke to me. He asked me to step outside. The boys were out there. I was to ask them in.

There was no problem about that. But for the two plainclothesmen, the street was deserted. The Aryan hadn't changed. I knew him by his T-shirt. The man the inspector'd had on Raymond was a Homicide Squad old-timer. I knew him from way back. The boys took over on the two goons. They cuffed them and patted them down. Neither was carrying a gun but both had mean looking knives. The knives looked razor sharp. Raymond's pockets also yielded two small, steel carpenter's clamps. Those would be an improvisation, but fitted to a finger and tightened slowly they could do a job. Thumb screws, after all, can't be picked up in any hardware store. At least these days they can't.

"You heard?" Jane asked.

"Every word," Schmitty said. "Every word and every move. We have the two of them dead to rights. We have them for breaking and entering. We have them for simple assault. We have them for threatening bodily harm.

We have them for attempted extortion. We don't need conspiracy, but we have them for that, too. Now all that is very nice, but it isn't much good to me. I'm a specialist and my specialty is homicide. I need somebody for Murder One."

"You don't pin that on us," Gibbons yelped.

"You know where we was," Raymond added.

"I know where everyone was," the inspector said. "And everybody has a sound alibi, everybody but you, Mrs. Dutton. You were here."

"Of course, I was here and I saw . . ."

Schmitty wasn't waiting for her to finish.

"You were here," he said. "It was your gun. It was your stocking. That was a cute idea, the sentimental journey into the past. When you thought that one up, you didn't know quite enough. You didn't know what the lab boys can do with a little hair, a little sweat, a little slobber. It was supposed to make it seem like one of these guys. It was the same kind of mask as they wore on the Sandringham job."

"Are you crazy?" Jane turned to me. "Your friend's crazy, George. I've had all I can take. Get him out of here. It's time I was left alone. God knows, I've suffered enough."

"Not nearly enough, Mrs. Dutton," Inspector Schmidt said. "That night at the hotel, Mrs. Gordon and Baggy got caught up in the thing because Mrs. Gordon's plane had been delayed. Your plane wasn't delayed. You were working the hotel that night. You were doing the rooms. You went out to stow your haul. You had a safe place for it away from the hotel. That was what took you out so late at night."

"I've never heard such outrageous nonsense."

"You came back and you ran into even bigger things
going in the lobby. I don't know how soon you came down
with the idea that you might have a piece of that, too, if
not the whole of it, but you worked it beautifully."

"George was there. He knows how absurd this is. I
didn't work anything."

"At the studio Baggy was separated from you. He
didn't see the way you worked on Dutton. It couldn't
have developed better for a dame who didn't want a husband. She just wanted the loot. Marrying a guy in jail.
That was the ideal marriage. You had the whole power of
the state to keep him in his place. Then when he got out,
you had to put up with him only for a while, only until
William Raymond had served out his term. That's the
way you had it timed. There was all that evidence that
made Raymond the murdering type. Raymond is free.
Bang! A man comes in the window with the stocking over
his face. He comes unarmed but that would be Raymond's way. Isn't he a craftsman, a guy who likes working with his hands? For him it would be strangulation or
a knife job, but strangulation or a knife wouldn't do for
you. For you it had to be a gun, but that would be all
right. It would be that Raymond came in the window;
but, with the gun lying ready to hand, he couldn't allow
himself the luxury of the handwork he liked. Dutton
might grab up the gun and get him. So he rides with ne-
cessity. He grabs up the gun himself and he shoots
Dutton."

"But I didn't," Raymond protested. "You just said it
yourself that I ain't done it."

"That's right," Schmitty said. "You ain't done it. It was
just going to look that way. She murdered her husband
and then she fired the second shot at the window. There

was nobody there, of course, but she needed the second shot. She'd heard about paraffin tests and, if paraffin tests show anything, what they show doesn't include telling whether the hand that held the gun fired it once or twice. She covered herself for the paraffin test."

She turned to me.

"George," she said. "You know it's all untrue. You know me. You knew Dutt. You know how I loved him. You saw how we were together."

"I knew Dutt," I said. "He was a good guy. For all the larceny he had in his soul, he was still a good guy."

"It isn't everybody's soul that has room for more than larceny," Schmitty said. "It's too bad he had to fall for a woman who had room for nothing else."

Later I asked the inspector what he'd found in the old records that opened it up for him.

"Nobody'd thought to question the truth of her statement that it was because of insomnia that she was walking at that hour of the morning," Schmitty said. "Somebody had been working upstairs, and if the woman who'd lost jewelry and money out of her room had reported it right instead of just stuffing it to the insurance company, someone might have asked. All her movements fitted too well. They've always fitted too well. She skipped out quick after the two of you were turned loose. So she wouldn't have to testify against him? No. She was off some place to fence her take from the rooms."

For the inspector the whole thing finished right there. The rest was up to the DA's men, to the judge, and the jury. His job done, Schmitty went on to other things. That has always been his way. For me, however, it wasn't so easy. In this one I was too closely involved. I followed the trial.

Jane was at her best in court. I knew her to be a great performer, but throughout the trial she was giving the performance of her life. She was so good that I more than half expected that she would have the jury snowed. At that, she must have come close. They took the better part of forever for their deliberations, but eventually they did come through with the guilty verdict.

The Sandringham loot has still not surfaced, but if I know Jane, she's doing a great job in the good behavior department. She'll be planning on serving only the minimum. She'll have all that lovely stuff waiting for her when she gets out.